"I knew this would happen."

Looking down at her, anger and frustration in his eyes, he said, "You're killing me, you know that? Killing me by inches, ripping my willpower to shreds." He sighed. "I want to see you again. No—I have to see you again...tonight."

"Tonight?" she echoed, dazed. "Like a...do you mean...a date?"

"Oh, God," he groaned, shaking his head. "Yes, a date—if that's what you want, a date."

He pulled back, releasing her, still shaking his head. "Turn me down," he begged. "Say no while you can."

"Never."

"Okay," he said, gazing at her with such intensity she felt weak. "But don't say I didn't warn you."

Dear Reader,

Welcome to Silhouette! Our goal is to give you hours of unbeatable reading pleasure, and we hope you'll enjoy each month's six new Silhouette Desires. These sensual, provocative love stories are both believable and compelling—sometimes they're poignant, sometimes humorous, but always enjoyable.

Indulge yourself. Experience all the passion and excitement of falling in love along with our heroine as she meets the irresistible man of her dreams and together they overcome all obstacles in the path to a happy ending.

If this is your first Desire, I hope it'll be the first of many. If you're already a Silhouette Desire reader, thanks for your support! Look for some of your favorite authors in the coming months: Stephanie James, Diana Palmer, Dixie Browning, Ann Major and Doreen Owens Malek, to name just a few.

Happy reading!

Isabel Swift
Senior Editor

SDRL-7/85

SUZANNE FORSTER
The Man at Ivy Bridge

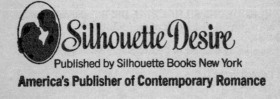

Silhouette Desire

Published by Silhouette Books New York

America's Publisher of Contemporary Romance

SILHOUETTE BOOKS
300 East 42nd St., New York, N.Y. 10017

Copyright © 1987 by Suzanne Forster

ISBN: 0-373-05327-4

First Silhouette Books printing January 1987

America's Publisher of Contemporary Romance

Printed in the U.S.A.

Books by Suzanne Forster

Silhouette Desire

Undercover Angel #215
Hot Properties #273
The Man at Ivy Bridge #327

SUZANNE FORSTER

started her writing career by accident. Literally. She took up writing while confined to bed after a car accident, and her first published book was discovered quite accidentally by an editor who read it while judging the finalists in the 1984 Romance Writers of America writing contest. Accidents do happen, but Ms. Forster's talent is the real key to her success.

To Tara Hughes, an editor every writer dreams of: tireless, commited and inspirational.

One

There he is," she whispered to the dust-streaked window-pane. Chloe Kates shivered with anticipation as the tall, dark-haired man materialized through the early-morning mist and hesitated at the shoreline to peer out over the foaming surf. His denim-clad legs formed a defiant triangle against the horizon as he pushed the sleeves of his fisherman's sweater up to his elbows and crossed his arms. Chloe's heart tapped out a Sousa march against her ribs.

She'd been watching him for two days now.

Since her arrival at the small, Maine seacoast resort motel the day before yesterday, she'd kept vigil at the window where, partially hidden by fraying drapes, she'd observed his every move.

Standing not more than fifty feet from her, he warned intruders away with the stony set of his shoulders. She'd only seen his face once, when he'd turned around abruptly, and she'd had to duck behind the curtain.

But sometimes once is enough.

Chloe inhaled a steadying breath. His shadowed features still haunted her. The glint in his eyes reminded her of a wolf intent on its prey.

Did he know she was watching?

He uncrossed his arms and, for a second, Chloe thought he was going to turn around again. When he didn't, she released her breath in a tight sigh. "Damn," she muttered. She almost wanted him to see her and finally put an end to the anxious waiting. She hadn't the courage to approach him and introduce herself. Breaching that angry, wind-whipped aura was beyond her mettle.

She tensed as he began to walk toward the sandy point that jutted out into the ocean. She knew from experience he would cover the quarter-mile distance quickly, then round the projection and disappear.

Gathering her courage, she slipped on a hooded, zip-up sweatshirt over her tattered Harvard T-shirt and faded jeans. At the bureau mirror, she stopped a moment to comb her fingers through the wild scatter of her coppery curls and grimace at her hopelessly cherubic face before she slipped out the door.

Still half expecting him to turn around, she stayed a safe distance behind him and hoped the wind and surf would muffle whatever noise she made. An Indian scout, she wasn't.

Her canvas sneakers tried to match the path his prints made in the hard-packed sand, and the effort it took made her realize how much larger his feet were than hers, how much longer his stride. Matching her footsteps to his became a momentary obsession, until a swooping sea gull dropped its shadow in her path, startling her before it whisked away. Its cry asked a plaintive question: *Why?* The chill mist held her in a forbidden caress. Why was she following this virtual stranger?

Because he resembled the man at ivy bridge?

Her heartbeat jumped tempo. She *must* be going crazy. This damp, dank place was shorting out her circuitry. All right, she admitted, the man's features *were* similar, especially those blood-chilling eyes, but was that a reason to pull up stakes and follow him to the ends of the earth?

As she refocused her sights on the striding form ahead, her thoughts flashed back to the writers' conference in Cape Cod where she'd seen him three weeks before. The fleeting brush of his dark eyes had stirred memories... haunting, half-formed images that told her he was connected to her past.

For several days afterward she'd tried to convince herself that the disturbing flashes of recall were unrelated to the man she'd momentarily caught sight of. But it was no use. His appearance had triggered a rush of déjà vu that no amount of logic could dispel.

She found out his name and even though it wasn't the name she sought, something urged her on. She learned he was a mystery writer and, with some difficulty, ferreted out that he'd taken a monthly rental in a motel an hour or so down the coast from Rockland, Maine. He was reclusive. He'd once been a poet.

But a spate of questions remained unanswered. Was he the man who, fourteen years ago, had turned her young life and the little town she lived in upside down? The man she'd seen on the bridge? She'd been twelve then, not quite a child, not yet a woman, that vulnerable time when a young girl's romantic imagination was stirring, ready to be awakened.

A shiver raised the fine hairs on her neck. Sara, her eighteen-year-old stepsister, had disappeared the same week

Chloe had first noticed him near their land. Had Sara run away as they said? Or had *he* had something to do with it?

Her quarry increased his pace, and she broke into a trot to keep up. A tangy, salty wind snapped at her chestnut hair. There were so many reasons to stop, to turn around, pack her bags and catch the first flight back to New York. Her struggling public-relations firm needed her! She couldn't expect her partner to carry on alone indefinitely.

Not only that, she reminded herself, it had been fourteen years since she'd seen the man in question. Considering the tens of thousands of tall men with dark hair and dark eyes, what were the chances she had the right one?

But she couldn't stop—for lots of reasons she didn't understand, and for one she did—her stepfather's recent illness. He'd summoned her to his hospital bedside to ask for her help in finding his daughter. She hadn't seen James Guthrie in more than a decade, and his pallid features had shocked her. She'd feared him as a child, even hated him at times, but ill as he was now, she couldn't deny his request.

A gull's sharp cry pulled her attention back to the man ahead of her. Uncanny, she thought, observing his deliberate stride. Even the way he walked triggered flashbacks. Was it memory or wishful thinking? The man she remembered had awakened her romantic imagination and more...he'd fascinated and frightened her.

The thought that she might have found him again set off a flurry of nervous anticipation. She increased her pace, aware of another sensation deep in her belly, a lurking tickle of fear. It should have warned her. Instead, it seemed to heighten the sense of urgency she felt.

As he rounded the point, she broke into a run, some part of her afraid he would vanish. Her hurried dash along the shoreline brought him back into her sights. He was ascending a ramp to a weather-beaten pier that looked as if the next wave would sweep it out to sea. By the time she reached the ramp, he stood at the end of the pier, his hands braced on the slatted railing, arms spread wide. As he stared off into the horizon, Chloe saw his shoulders rise and fall with a sigh. A troubled man, she concluded, an odd resonance brushing her heart.

At the pier's anguished creaking, she wanted to warn him to be careful, but almost as soon as she'd talked herself out of the idea, she saw him do something extraordinary. Staring down into the water some twenty feet below he pulled off his sweater and bent over the wooden railing, so far over that Chloe heard herself gasp.

What was he doing? Was there something in the water? she wondered, squinting to see where he was looking. She scanned the area carefully but detected nothing in the inlet's murky depths other than surface ruffles built by the gusty winds. Certainly nothing to get excited about.

His next move made her wonder at his sanity.

Straightening, he hoisted a leg over the railing and planted his foot on the narrow outside ledge, then shifted his weight and began to follow suit with the second foot.

She cocked her head, confused. What *was* he doing? And then a crashing realization slammed her heart against her ribs. He was going to jump!

She bolted up the ramp, a scream forming as she sprinted over the wooden planks.

"No!" she cried. "Don't do it!" But the wind caught her words and tore them away.

The man didn't hear her. He seemed oblivious, even to the shaking pier, and he struggled to free his pant leg, which had snagged on the wood. Chloe's feet flew over the swaying structure. "Don't do it!" she pleaded as she got closer to him. With an urgent lunge, she caught his foot before he could pull it over.

Wobbling precariously, he looked around, startled, aware of her for the first time.

"D-don't do this," she cried, gripping his foot and tugging with all her strength. What would a crisis counselor say? "Where there's life there's hope!" she ad-libbed frantically. *"Please—"* She hugged his foot. "There's so much to live for!"

His wordless astonishment faded to annoyance. Dark eyes narrowing curiously, he gave his foot a determined tug.

Chloe held on for dear life, her fingernails scraping across the white canvas Adidas sneakers. "Oh please, no," she whispered, digging in her heels and gritting her teeth.

"For God's sake, let go of me," he said, his incredulous frown deepening as he tugged again then shook his foot to disengage her. Chloe felt his shoe wobble and her grip along with it. In a flash of blinding insight, she foresaw the awful consequences of his loosening footwear, but her leverage and backward momentum were too much. Let go? *She couldn't!*

The shoe gave. Hanging on to it helplessly, she lurched into reverse, skittering away from him, arms flailing, tennis shoe flying, feet scrambling to change gears. The opposite railing stopped her tailspin short as she hit the rotten wood with a soft *thummk* and a startled cry.

The railing heaved a groan of protest. Sickening crackles resounded as the slats began to give away. With a shrill scream, Chloe grabbed for something, anything!

The slat she caught broke off, and the entire railing sagged with her weight. Dear God, she'd had nightmares about dropping off the edge of the earth into a watery abyss, and now it was coming true! She saw herself hurtling, hurtling twenty feet to the dank water below.

Her breath left her as a wrenching force gripped her arms, and she felt herself being jerked upright. Powerful hands snatched her back and set her on her feet.

Her legs wanted to fold like a portable chair's, but he wouldn't let them. Steadied by his strong, sure-handed grip on her arms, she fought to catch up with her racing heart.

A moment later, a shock wave of delayed realization trembled through her. She was *safe*. Oh, thank goodness. The sun was in its heaven, the sea below—and with a little help from her dark-haired friend here, Chloe Kates was safe and dry on a creaky dock.

Friend? Still shivering, she opened her eyes and blinked. A stretch of tanned skin gradually came into focus.

Realizing her clearing field of vision was somewhere between his chin and his chest, she stared at the dark body hair that crept over tanned collarbones and into the hollow at the base of his neck. Unequal to exploring any higher, or lower, she simply gave in to her body's lead and sagged with relief. He'd caught her. Everything was going to be all right.

His arms wrapped her in a warm, powerful embrace, one hand spanning the space just below her shoulder blades, the other smoothing her tangled hair.

Her cheek rested against the very same furry chest she'd witnessed earlier. "Hello," she rasped as soon as her voice would cooperate. "Name's . . . Chloe."

"Chloe." He murmured her name as though it might shed some light on what had just happened. "Do you always introduce yourself this dramatically?"

"Sorry," she whispered, still nestled against him. "I was supposed to save your life, not you mine."

His soft laugh vibrated through her. "Next time I'll be sure my shoelaces are tied." His hand was engaged in wonderfully soothing ministrations to her disorderly hair, her pulsing temple, her flushed cheek.

Easing back, she looked up into eyes that were blacker than a moonless night. Breath caught high in her throat, rushed out, then caught again. Was this the man she'd seen? The man at ivy bridge?

She searched a face that shouted of reckless discontent, it's harsh lines only briefly tempered by concern. His angular features were roughened by the shadow of a heavy beard and carelessly bordered by a dark mane of hair.

Her mind faltered—it's not him, this man is too tall, too lean, his features too stormy—but her senses, her body, dismissed all her objections. Her pulse beat said yes. Her heart rate said yes....

His narrowed gaze brought her back. "You okay now?" he questioned.

"You were going to jump," she said softly. "Why?"

"Jump?" The word was followed by surprised laughter. "You thought— Well, I guess that explains your impetuous attraction to my shoe."

He wasn't going to jump? "What were you—"

"I was rescuing my sunglasses. They dropped off yesterday, and I gave them up for lost, but this morning there they were, dangling from a crossbeam, and—"

"Please," she advised quietly, "buy yourself another pair."

"Sounds like a good idea," he conceded. "Unfortunately, they don't make glasses like that anymore." His brows flattened. "You sure you're okay?"

She shook her head, reluctantly disengaging herself from him, and held up a smarting, splinter-ridden palm.

"Uh-oh," he said and whistled softly, his mouth lifting in a wonderfully crooked grin. "You'll never play the accordion again."

A surprised gurgle escaped her. "Such a tragic waste of talent." She sighed, deadpan. "Lawrence Welk's loss."

His eyes returned to her, and his smile deepened.

Whoever he was, she decided, staring up at him, he *was* something. Falling-down gorgeous! Could this be the same mysterious man she'd been watching for forty-eight hours?

Proceed with caution, her mind whispered.

Nudging the advice aside, she smiled, too. "How 'bout you?"

"Hmm?" His eyebrows knitted.

"Oh," she faltered, flushing slightly. "I meant you aren't hurt are you?" She glanced gingerly at his muscular arms, his hands. "No splinters ... or anything?"

Eyes twinkling, he hunched his shoulders. "Nah, I'm tough."

Watching as he pulled on his sweater and put on his sneaker, she realized how relieved she was that he hadn't been about to do what she'd thought he'd been about to do.

"What's your name?" she asked nonchalantly. After her questionable first impression it might be wiser to make this look like a chance meeting.

"Nathanial Cutter," he mumbled, occupied. A moment later, he was back, inspecting her wounded hand. "I think it can be saved," he diagnosed, straight-faced, then winked engagingly. "Let's go find a pair of tweezers and I'll operate."

They departed the pier, side by side, Chloe struggling to keep pace with his long-legged stride until finally she was breathless. "Could we take this a little slower?" she suggested.

Noting her rapid footwork, he laughed again, soft and husky. "Can't have my patient expiring from exhaustion." He paused for a moment, staring at her with such intense concentration she felt her pulse beat waver. *Does he remember? Does he know who I am?*

But something told her the lights in his dark eyes were not motivated by recognition. They were curious, subtly analytical and very, *very* sensual.

She averted her gaze. "Where are we going, Doctor?" she asked, wishing her voice wasn't quite so breathy.

"Room 15, the Sunrise motel. I do all my emergency surgeries there."

She felt a quick tug in her stomach. "Wonderful," she said with feigned aplomb. "I'm staying there, too. I'll be able to do my post-op convalescence next door in room 14."

His head came around abruptly, distance in his eyes. No one had to tell her something was wrong. She could see the wariness growing in him, could almost feel it.

"How long have you been there?" he questioned, continuing to walk.

"Just a couple of days," she offered, wondering foolishly if that was the right answer. "You?"

"Not long."

Two words had never sounded so final.

The rest of their half-mile journey was completed in silence while Chloe's curiosity ran like an imp out of control. Her mind cartwheeled with questions about the insular man who walked beside her as if he didn't give a damn that his jeans had a tear at the calf and that one of his shirttails emerged rebelliously from under his sweater.

He was older than her twenty-six years, she knew immediately, and wondered by exactly how much. Eight years, she speculated, nine? *That would put him at about the right age.* His stride was purposeful, his body lithe and supplely muscled, but his eyes signaled trouble. Beyond their temporary diversion with her, they were the searching, hungry eyes of a malcontent.

His pensive profile held her in thrall.

"What is he thinking about?" she wondered so fiercely that she actually asked it aloud.

He turned his head sharply.

Instinctively, she drew up a hand.

Gradually his features surrendered some of their guardedness. His eyes glanced over her, brushing her with a fleeting spark. "I was thinking," he said, "about temptation and opportunity... and how to tell them apart."

Seated at the kitchenette table of Nathanial's motel room, Chloe drew in a breath when he took her hand. "Be gentle, Doctor," she said, not entirely flip.

And he was, incredibly, as he removed the slivers from her red-welted palm.

Several times Chloe found it necessary to remind herself why she'd followed him to Maine, and even then the caution only held for a minute or two. There was something utterly distracting in the way he cradled her hand, almost as though it might be the most delicate thing he'd ever touched.

His capacity for gentleness mesmerized her.

Fascinated by the seeming contradictions in his nature, she sat wordlessly, shivering as she realized how totally she'd entrusted herself to the man who knelt beside her.

He'd rolled up his sleeves, revealing forearms dusted with sable hair. Watching his long agile fingers work magic with the tweezers, she smiled comtemplatively. These could be the hands of a classical pianist, a neurosurgeon, a gifted sculptor. They could be anything, she realized... even the hands of the phantom from her past.

When the last tiny lance was freed, he cleansed the area with soap and water and studied his handiwork soberly. His fingers brushed lightly, exploring the slight swellings. And then, without warning, he raised her palm to his lips as if to heal each wound.

Chloe's breath went high and thready.

"Kiss and make it better?" she said, trying to laugh, her heart in her throat. Soft and cool, his mouth touched each tiny mark, shimmering over her palm, the roughness of his unshaved jaw gently abrading her flesh. Lord, but it was startling, so startling she could feel her toes curl.

She felt a surge of delicious fear as he stopped, letting a beat pass before he raised his head to look at her. Time seemed to slow to half tempo and eddy around her as she acknowledged the most starkly beautiful eyes she'd ever seen.

His hand came up to touch her cheek, a whisper of skin against skin, and the contact, even in its gentleness, jarred her. She closed her eyes and wished herself away, far away, anywhere, somewhere, *safe*.

"Look at me," he said, his voice a husky whisper.

The air breathed with expectancy as she hesitated, half-raising her lashes, seeing him through a gauzy veil. The area behind him faded to a soft watercolor blur as his dark eyes seemed to reach out from the past and touch her. They were irresistible, hypnotic. For a moment she could almost feel the beating heart of the breathless young girl she had once been.

"You're lovely," he said, the quiet reverence in his words drawing her back to reality. "Your face has the cleanest lines I've ever seen." Visually tracing the oval curves from cheek to chin, he added, "The contours are flawless, the skin tones rich and true."

"Flawless...?" she questioned. "No—I'm not even pretty, really."

"I didn't say pretty," he stated gently. "I said clean and true."

He stood up then, offered her his hand.

Acutely aware of him, she knew that even the touch of his fingers was more contact than she could handle at the moment. "No, I—" She pushed back, chair and all, as she rose. Brushing at her clothes, she stepped away, giving herself the distance she needed to regroup.

Outside the strange aura of energy he gave off, she remembered her mission. She'd come here for a reason. A deep breath steadied her. She edged a look at him. "Haven't we met somewhere before?"

"Haven't we—" He exhaled a soft gust of laughter. "I thought they'd retired that line years ago."

"No, it's not a line." Without thinking, she moved closer and presented her face to him. "I, uh, do I look at all familiar to you?" Her heart quickened expectantly.

"Chloe, if I'd ever met you before," he said, his eyes sincere in their scrutiny, "I wouldn't have forgotten."

Their eyes held, and she felt that irresistible energy again. It was the oddest, most indescribable sensation of light rushing and sliding inside her, wind chimes and whispers beckoning softly in the distance.

"Oh—" She lost whatever she'd planned to say next in a hushed intake of air.

His lips parted and she found herself entranced. Their carved shadings and texture made her think of the timeless lines of classic sculpture. A low thrill swept her as she remembered how they'd felt on her palm. From somewhere an errant breeze, cool and light, caressed her face, her mouth. *What would it be like to kiss him?* she wondered.

She felt a sweet jolt of anticipation as he took her hand. They moved to each other, their eyes locked, and then she let hers drift shut as he bent toward her. Warm breath feathered her lower lashes. His mouth touched her parted lips, and she felt a descending sensation, and with it, a rush of giddiness.

The kiss deepened, a moment out of time.

Chloe was lost in his taste and his scent and the feel of his mouth on hers. The pleasure swirling inside her elicited a honey-sweet languor that made her want to soften against him. Breathy sounds of pure appreciation hovered in her throat.

A feather traced the arc of her neck...his breath, his fingers? "I know who you are," he whispered.

The words floated in her mind, unheeded for several seconds before she realized what they meant. And then the thunder cracked, a bolt that brought her eyes wide open. She took a step back. "You do?"

Staring down at her, he nodded.

The next moments stretched endlessly. She was barely aware of him reaching out to touch her hair, taking a russet curl between his fingers. He said, his voice husky, "'I met a lady in the meads. Full beautiful, a faery's child; Her hair was long, her foot was light, And her eyes were wild.'"

"Faery's child?" Her heart was beating so erratically it took her a moment to put it all together. "Keats?" She looked up at him, her voice light with disbelief. "You mean— You were talking about a poem?"

He nodded slowly. "A poem. About you, I think."

Her breath caught. She'd thought he meant— Trying to smile, she mumbled inanely, "Thank you, but Keats was a couple of years before my time."

"Hey," he said, tilting her chin up, concerned, "is something wrong?"

She pulled away, shaking her head and realizing what she should have known before. Nathanial Cutter was dangerous. He could throw a woman off the track with a word, a glance. In the course of a morning, he'd saved her life, brought her to his motel room, performed surgery on her hand, kissed her breathless and she still didn't know anything more about him now than when she had arrived in Maine. She could hardly keep track of why she was here!

Collecting herself, she gave him an appraising stare. There was only one way to find out what she had to know. *Ask.* But did she put it to him straight, or did she try an angle? Fortifying herself with a quick breath, she took a chance. "I hope this doesn't sound too presumptuous, but is . . . is Nathanial Cutter your real name?"

Was that a spark of recognition she saw, a fleeting instant of acknowledgement? She couldn't be sure. His gaze was narrowing, his eyes losing their warmth.

He studied her as though he could, by sheer effort of will, see inside her mind, read her intentions. And then he turned away to face the motel room's small kitchenette. His fingers riffled through his hair before he came back around slowly, his expression wary, faintly puzzled. "What are you—a reporter?"

"No," she said quickly. The change taking place in him was tangible, passion was being replaced by something increasingly hard and impenetrable.

"What then? What do you want?"

Did she dare tell him why she was here? *Not unless you want to be thrown out like yesterday's trash, girl,* she warned. Tension rippled clear to her fingertips as her body signaled its instinctive knowledge: Nathanial Cutter *was* dangerous.

"I'm a fan, that's all," she said, her voice hushed.

"A *fan?*"

The edge in his voice told her she'd made a mistake. Considering her options, she realized if she backed off now, she'd lose whatever ground she'd made, as well as any chance of gaining his trust. "Yes, a fan," she said deliberately. "Is that so hard to believe?"

He turned away again, stony and silent, much the way she'd seen him that morning when he'd stood in the mists facing the ocean. "Yes," he said finally, "it is."

When he faced her again, his expression was thoughtful. "I'm a private man. I don't apologize for that. And I don't have much use for *fans*. But let's say you are one," he acknowledged, a quiet challenge in his eyes. "Tell me then— I'm curious about something. What did you think of the abduction scene in *Siren's Song*?"

Aware that he had moved toward her, hesitating not five feet from her, she steadied herself, desperate not to let him know she hadn't read *Siren's Song*, or any of his work. "I— I found it ... frighteningly real."

"Really?" His voice dropped low, harsh. "I like liars even less than fans, Chloe, or whatever your name is. *There's no abduction scene in that book*."

Instinctively she edged back, glancing at the door. "I—I must have been confused," she explained. "It was another book."

"Damn, but you're a clever piece of business," he murmured, nodding, his voice gruff and almost appreciative. "That bit of drama on the dock was first-rate." Appraising her, his features hardened. "Who are you?"

Ignoring him, Chloe continued to edge back, her instincts sharpened with surges of adrenaline. *She had to know.* "Did you ever live in upstate New—"

With two strides he caught her, his hand urging her chin up, his eyes threatening dark consequences. *"No more questions."*

For a breathless moment he hovered near, a pulse beat from her lips, his gaze burning a message of peril along the nerve endings that honeycombed her spine. And then, just as abruptly, he released her. "I think you'd better get out of here."

Faltering, she backed away, hesitated for an instant, then turned and fled. As the door closed behind her, she took several shaky steps and then slumped against the shingled wall of the motel. Tension released from her in a trembling sigh.

Her head spun with confusion. What had just happened? And why? She felt as if she'd been dealing with not one man, but two. He'd been eloquent, gentler than any man she'd ever known...and then, not ten minutes later, his eyes had ignited and he'd turned menacing. Closing her eyes, she saw nothing but his dark fire, the way the sun blinds you long after you turn away. *What had she blundered into?*

Two

Several minutes later, still shaken and confused by Cutter's reaction, Chloe hesitated at the door of her motel room. She couldn't go inside yet. She needed space to think and breathe.

Beyond the small, twenty-unit building to the south, a path wound up along the rocky bluffs overlooking the shoreline. Chloe reached it in minutes.

She slowly walked along the trail, staring out at the horizon with unfocused eyes as she tried to make sense of Cutter's volatile behavior. He was a writer, a private man by his own admission, but surely that couldn't account for his mood changes, or the way he'd tossed her out on her ear. Writers were a difficult breed, no one understood that better than she, but this man...

She hesitated, aware for the first time of the chill breeze, the gooseflesh on her arms. This man had something to hide.

Hugging herself, she caught sight of a weather-beaten bench nestled between clustered rocks and shrubbery. She reached it in a few quick strides, settling in, bringing her knees to her chest in a body tuck against the cold.

Gradually her shivering eased, and she saw all at once the breathtaking seascape stretched before her. The ocean looked as though an artist had chopped it out with a palette knife. Low in the sky, alabaster rays pierced gray haze; directly above her, mounds of cloud upon cloud glowed with a golden fringe, backlit by the risen sun.

Untucking her legs, Chloe let out a sigh. The answers she sought were in her past, locked in that single catastrophic week of her childhood...but more than that, the answers were all bound up in the secrets of the Guthries, the reclusive family she'd struggled so hard to feel part of after her mother's death.

Why had her mother married James Guthrie? What had she found to love in the forbidding textiles magnate? Chloe felt a flash of sadness, remembering the skiing accident that had taken her mother's life on the first day of her Gstaad honeymoon with Guthrie. Just eleven years old, Chloe'd been left in the sole care of a harsh, embittered man.

She'd spent two years at Northpointe, Guthrie's somber English Tudor-style mansion in upstate New York, a time that shimmered in her mind like a mirage...memories that vanished when approached. The few times she had been able to call the past up, the events had seemed almost surreal, a waking dream peopled with shadows and fleeting images.

A shudder sent the gooseflesh prickling down her arms.

But that had all changed three weeks ago...when her brief and fatal glimpse of Nathanial Cutter at the writers' conference in Cape Cod began triggering flashes of recall. Since that day, random details seemed to spring out at her from everywhere—splashes of color, certain sounds, even innocently printed words quivered like divining rods, tapping at her memory.

Sometimes it felt as though debris from a shipwreck was floating to the surface, bits and pieces taking shape in her mind. Seeing Cutter had started it, and her recent visit to her stepfather's bedside had acted like a catalyst, accelerating the process.

And now, since she'd arrived in Maine, whole chunks of that lost week of her childhood had come back with such clarity it left her breathless. She remembered the day Sara, Guthrie's graceful, soft-spoken daughter, arrived home from college in the middle of term, summoned by her father. Distraught, Sara had locked herself in her room after a hushed, urgent argument with Guthrie, and had never gone back to school.

Chloe had always admired her stepsister and longed to make contact, but Sara's quiet manner and ethereal beauty made her seem unapproachable. And she'd so rarely been home. After the fight with her father, Sara had withdrawn completely to her own inaccessible world.

The argument. *Was that when it all started?* Chloe's mind quickened as she remembered the events that followed Sara's return to Northpointe. Sliding down, she rested her head against the bench back and shut her eyes.

Instead of resisting, the memories beckoned, pulling at her so irresistibly it almost frightened her. A shiver rippled through her as she let herself go, let herself dissolve into the past and become that twelve-year-old girl again....

Running, running like a frightened animal, she'd dropped and burrowed into the covering bower of an ivy-wrapped bridge. The high, quick racing of her heart beat in her throat as she rose from her crouch to peer over the wooden railing. Eyes as wide as searchlights, she tracked the approaching shadowy figure.

He'd appeared out of the forest across the creek, materializing through the dawn haze, startling her so badly she'd instinctively darted for cover.

He was heading right for her hiding place, the footbridge that spanned the creek bordering their land. Was he coming to Northpointe? What could he want? They never had visitors here. Her stepfather despised strangers, despised most people he knew, too.

As he neared, Chloe crouched again and crept to a spot alongside the bridge, waiting for the sound of his footsteps on the pine planks as he crossed over. As the silence lengthened, fear rose inside her. Where was he? Did she dare look again?

She did look, her heart trembling, and found him gone, gone so completely that she was sure he'd never been there, sure she'd imagined him. She searched the area again, and her shoulders fell with a sigh. Was he only a dream? Just like all the other inventions of her imagination?

Returning to the house, she escaped to the dim, chilly confines of her room, curled up and let her mind drift away. Daydreams eased her loneliness, sweet reveries full of all the things she missed and longed for—her mother's gentle voice, even the laughter and whispers of old school friends sharing secrets about boys and clothes and their glowing future prospects.

That night, lost in another kind of reverie, Chloe was a captive princess, beautiful and fragile, languishing in her confinement, dying a slow death of the heart and spirit…a cageling princess pining for release.

The next morning brought a misty sunrise—and an extraordinary event. Chloe's mysterious stranger reappeared from the woods across the creek, and she knew immediately that he was no dream. He came into view several more times over the next few days, always surreptitiously, always watching the Tudor mansion as though he expected its massive doors to open and a host of angels—or devils—to emerge.

Chloe began to discover him at other places on the estate grounds, too: the deserted stables, the overgrown rose gardens, lurking by the rusted tool sheds. Sometimes he appeared and was gone so quickly, she wasn't sure if she'd seen a man or a shadow. Careful to remain unseen herself, she stalked him with dogged fascination, never daring to get close enough for a good look. And never telling anyone of her discovery.

Who would she have told anyway? she wondered late one night, struggling with her conscience. Sara never came out of her room, and James Guthrie, suspicious of even his own household staff, would undoubtedly have stalked and shot the intruder himself. Perhaps the housekeeper or her handyman husband? Before giving up, Chloe briefly considered even her year-round tutor, a thin, cheerless woman. No, she decided, every one of them could be counted upon to assume he was up to no good. They might even panic and call the police.

Chloe felt sure the stranger was up to something, too, something secret and wonderful. Without understanding how or why, she sensed a special purpose in him . . . and she had to know what it was.

The next morning, just as dawn broke, she slipped unseen from a side door of the house and raced toward the creek, her bare feet shiny and wet from the dewy grass.

She stopped when the bridge came into view, arrested by something, a quiver in the air, a presence she felt but couldn't see, and then she saw him through the ivy bowers, standing at the railing, illumined by a shaft of filtered sunlight. As always, he observed Northpointe.

She moved closer cautiously, drawn to him, her eyes rushing over his absorbed profile. Was this the same man? He looked different somehow, magical. His hair was the color of the foothills at sunset—a rich, near-black hue. And his eyes, they were dark, too.

She edged closer, recklessly intrigued, certain his eyes must be as black as midnight and keenly aware that if he turned and saw her she'd have nowhere to run.

Bathed by the latticed brilliance of the rising sun, dappled in gold, he had the singular gaze of a man on a mission, a dreamer, a conqueror. Chloe paused, and in that one, shimmering instant, she believed, *wanted to believe*, he'd come there for her... to rescue her from her terrible loneliness.

The giddy, wistful thought took possession of her heart and mind. Entranced, she felt a pulse thrumming in her temples, racing in her veins. Her throat warmed with a spreading flush as she walked toward the bridge, openly now, expecting him to notice her at any moment. What would she do when he did? What would she say?

She froze as he whirled around, frozen like a cat caught in the glare of headlights. Stunned, expectant, she watched him turn and walk off the bridge. Before she could speak or move, he'd disappeared into the trees.

He hadn't seen her...?

Or he hadn't cared. Her throat caught in a swallow. Eyelids lowering, dampening with a sharp sting, she felt so young and lost, a hopeless child.

How dared he not see her when she'd seen nothing else but *him* for days? Impulsively, she began to follow him, running over the bridge, faltering to a halt as she entered the dank, lightless chamber of soaring evergreens.

She looked around her, alarmed by the encroaching shadows and the sudden snap of a branch overhead. Stumbling through the underbrush, she remembered how many times her stepfather had warned her never to leave the grounds. "They kidnap the children of wealthy families," he'd said, staring past her at unseen ghosts, neglecting to explain who "they" were.

A small clearing came into view and Chloe started for it, desperate to escape the darkness. A branch cracked behind her, then another and another in urgent, brittle succession. Someone was following her! She ran, her heart slamming against her chest, panic grasping at her like unseen fingers.

A tree branch loomed up; she veered away, but the next one caught her by the shoulder, knocking the breath out of her, tumbling her head over heels until she landed, facedown, gasping out a cry of alarm.

When she tried to pull herself up, he was there, standing in the shadows, his eyes catching light, milk-white as a wolf's glare in the moonlight.

A crazy, mindless fear iced her veins. Terrorized, she tried to drag herself away as he moved toward her, bending over her like a hovering demon, his arms outstretched. A scream tore from her throat and died, muffled by his gloved hand.

"Be quiet," he warned softly. Quiet? Chloe's heart roared in her ears. She flailed and twisted as he lifted her into his arms and began to move deeper into the forest. "Nobody's going to hurt you," he promised, catching both her wrists and holding them immobile.

She squeezed her eyes shut, and dizziness spun like tiny whirling pinwheels in her head. When she opened them, wincing, the world seemed lighter, the trees thinner, and then, miraculously, they were out of the forest. *He was carrying her back to the bridge.*

He set her down on the wooden planks in the pale sunlight, kneeling to support her with an arm behind her shoulders. "You'll be all right," he assured her. "You've had a little scare, that's all."

She drooped against him, her breathing rapid and thready.

"What's your name?" he asked after a moment, his husky, resonant tones rousing her.

"Chloe," she said, looking up at him. His were black as midnight. She would never forget them.

"Chloe," he repeated thoughtfully. "Yes, it's perfect."

Muted light caressed his compelling features...and Chloe's fear gradually gave way to wonderment. Was it him? Was he really holding her, looking down at her with such concern? Her heart lightened and tiptoed up into her throat.

"What's your name?" she asked finally.

"Joshua," he said, smiling. "It's Joshua, but don't tell anyone."

The glow from his eyes seemed to fill her with light. She felt strange and shimmery, as luminous as stardust. For a fleeting instant, she experienced an uncontrollable swell of happiness, an inexpressible kind of joy that threatened to cut off her breathing. Pressing both hands to her chest, she tried to capture the wonder of it all, for something told her she might never feel this way again.

A moment later, much too soon, he took his arm away, and Chloe felt a cold shock of air across her shoulder blades. She stared up at him, longing suffusing her green eyes, her throat full of the need to say things beyond her understanding.

"Innocence," he murmured, a roughened tenderness in his voice. "Innocence of heart." His eyes darkened for an instant, sparkling with amused, compassionate lights, and

Chloe thought she glimpsed a flash of wonder and longing before he looked away.

After a moment, he glanced down at her again and touched a forefinger to her cheek in a light caress. She shyly averted her gaze....

And he was gone, vanished in a eye blink, just as before.

She waited there all day, resting against the railing, oblivious to the calls from the house. Shutting her eyes, she squeezed them tight, and with all the energy she could gather, tried to bring him back. She didn't quite understand why, but to her waiting heart, it seemed the most important thing in her life that he come back for her. And he would, she knew it.

She held on stubbornly even as darkness settled around her. Huddled and freezing, she darted out of sight when the handyman tromped over the bridge, waving his flashlight and calling her name.

Much later, blue with cold and frightened by the night's lonely cries, she finally gave up her vigil. Stricken with disappointment, she approached the house, pausing in confusion as it came into full view. The mansion was ablaze with light. The Guthries were up? A lump lodged in Chloe's throat. Because of her?

She pushed tentatively on the heavy doors and gasped as they suddenly swung open. Cursing and muttering incoherently, the handyman caught Chloe's arm and pulled her inside.

"Where have you been?" the housekeeper wailed. "Sara's been taken! We thought you'd been, too."

James Guthrie clattered down the winding stairway and strode the length of the hallway, marching down on Chloe like a huge, cloaked devil. "What do you know about this?" he snarled.

"Nothing," Chloe breathed.

"Where the hell have you been?" he lashed out.

"I, uh," she said, faltering, looking down at her torn clothing and bruises. She knew she ought to tell him everything, but a gripping, unnamed fear stopped her. "I fell and hurt myself," she rasped. "I can't—I can't remember what happened. I think I must have fainted."

Guthrie turned his rage on the housekeeper next, berating her for calling the police.

"Your door was locked, sir," she pleaded, cowering. "You didn't answer my calls. I didn't know what else to do."

When the police arrived, Chloe learned that Sara's window had been found wide open. An overturned chair and shattered vase indicated signs of a struggle, but none of Sara's clothes or personal possessions had been touched and, oddest of all, no one in the house had been awakened by the noise.

"If it's a kidnapping, the guy can't have gotten far," a policeman observed. "Let's put the dogs on him. They'll hunt him down."

"They'll get him," another muttered under his breath. "Rip him apart."

Listening, Chloe began to tremble. A sick feeling filled her stomach. It couldn't be the man at the bridge, *not Joshua*. He wouldn't have done such a thing.

Her head snapped up as one of the policemen, a detective, approached her.

"Did you see or hear anything suspicious out there?" the detective asked, his pupils tiny as the pricking end of a needle.

"No," she told him, her heart beginning to pound.

Two other policemen joined them, all three watching her. "Was anybody with you?" one of them asked.

Chloe felt blood heat her face. Everyone seemed to have turned toward her now, even her stepfather. She dropped her eyes, and finally, her heart thumping painfully, she shook her head.

But it wasn't enough. The detective wanted to hear her statement. "I didn't—" she vowed, her voice faint. "I didn't see anyone."

After a long, horrible moment he turned away. They all turned away, done with her.

Chloe caught her hands at her stomach, about to be sick.

That night she dreamed again and again that Joshua was waiting for her on the bridge. Each time she tried desperately to reach him, and each time he disappeared. She woke up exhausted, confused, wandering the house, finally arriving at Sara's empty room where she hovered in the doorway, filled with a vague, rising dread.

In the days and weeks that followed there was no news of Sara Guthrie. James Guthrie quickly and thoroughly squelched the police investigation and press coverage, and brought in private detectives to search for his daughter.

Despite the rumors that Sara had been abducted, no ransom note ever came. Other rumors surfaced, increasingly morbid predictions that Chloe couldn't accept. The housekeeper believed Sara had been drugged and sold to a prostitution ring; her husband thought she'd been assaulted and murdered.

But Chloe's tutor held a completely different view. "Sara's run away to be with her lover," Chloe overheard her whispering to the housekeeper one morning not long after the incident, "the young man she met at school...."

Sara's lover?

A wave crashed against the rocks like a low clap of thunder. Chloe's eyes opened, and she sat up abruptly. How could she have forgotten that whispered conversation between her tutor and the housekeeper? Had it been swallowed up in the intervening years?

Closing her eyes, she tried to quiet the rush of noise in her head, and after a moment, the whirling fragments began to come together, to coalesce into meaning. The emotional conflict had been more than a twelve-year-old could handle. Yes, Chloe realized, slowly nodding her head. The trauma of Sara's disappearance, the confusion of her own motives for protecting Joshua, the knowledge that Sara and Joshua might have been lovers. She hadn't been able to face it. She'd had to deny it, to bury it. *God, she could hardly face it now.*

She took a deep breath and pressed her palms flat against the wooden slats of the bench. She'd been grateful to escape when Guthrie had sent her away the week after her thirteenth birthday, first to a boarding school in Vermont, then on to finishing school and college. At her own request, she'd never returned to Northpointe.

The young man she met at school, her mind whispered, refusing to be sidetracked by any other thoughts. How had the tutor known Sara had a young man at school? If she was right, *it explained everything.* The chair, the broken vase—overturned in their haste to get away, of course. They hadn't even had time to take Sara's clothes.

Chloe sprang up and started down the path toward the motel. Could Nathanial Cutter be Joshua? She had to know. Her feet hit the packed dirt with an urgent slapping sound. Even if he had been Sara's lover, *even if he still was,* she had to know. She would find a way to deal with the truth whatever it was.

Negotiating the winding path, she recalled the moment at James Guthrie's hospital bedside two weeks ago when he'd asked her if she'd ever been contacted by Sara. She hadn't, and told him so honestly, but afterward, when Guthrie'd become too weak to talk, his assistant, Gordon Browne, had drawn her aside.

"It's his heart," Browne told her. "He's desperate to find his daughter, so if you know anything about her, anything at all—" He'd gone on, pressing for information, but something furtive in his manner warned Chloe against revealing the stranger she'd seen on the grounds.

She'd come away from the hospital with the nagging feeling that Browne and Guthrie knew more than they'd told her, and another stronger hunch that Sara Guthrie was still alive.

That night Chloe had made a decision. Nat Cutter was her only link. She would go to Maine and find him....

Breaking into a jog, Chloe let her mind work. Finding Cutter had been the easy part—now she had to get past his guard. Questions made him defensive. Her breath came faster, keeping pace with her feet. Answers, then. She wouldn't ask, she'd tell him—*yes*, she'd tell him everything. Once she'd spilled out the whole story he'd realize he had nothing left to hide.

As the motel came into sight, she eased up a little, aware of a possible flaw in her plan. She wasn't high on Cutter's list of favorite people right now. What if he wouldn't listen to her? Reaching the paved walkway in front of the motel, she slowed down.

Her first tentative knock went unanswered. She tried again, feeling an odd mixture of relief and disappointment at the silence. He wasn't home.

The partially opened curtains caught her eye. One cautious look into the murky room told her she'd been wrong. He *was* home. Leaning against the doorjamb of the room's small hallway, he held the telephone receiver to his ear with a fist. He looked angry. A half-filled highball glass sat on the dresser top next to an open bottle of Scotch.

Cutter shook his head, gestured, apparently arguing with the caller. She winced as the receiver slammed down and he whisked up the glass. He took a long swallow.

Bad timing, she realized, ready to slip away.

A gasp hovered in her throat as the curtains jerked open. God, he was right there on the other side of the pane—glowering at her! She froze as the door banged open and he loomed in the doorway.

"What do you want?" he asked, his voice low and rough, the glass in his hand.

"I wanted to—" *Incredibly bad timing.* "To apologize," she said quickly. As his glower began to fade, she rushed on. "It was rude of me to be so—well, there's no other word for it—so nosy this morning. It's just that—"

The apology lodged in her throat. Why was he suddenly looking at her like that, with such rapt concentration as if he'd noticed something for the first time?

"Now I know who you remind me of," he said thickly.

"Who?" she breathed, edging a look at his glass. How much had he drunk?

"A woman—" He drained the Scotch and began walking toward her. "No, not a woman, a temptress . . . from an old Welsh myth."

"Myth?" She exhaled the word and cut it off in a flash of anger. That was twice he'd made her think he knew who she was. Was he purposely baiting her? "I'm not interested in poetry or myths, Mr. Cutter, I'm—"

His empty glass hit the concrete and shattered.

She veered back, screaming as he caught her wrist and dragged her out of the path of the broken fragments.

"Maybe you *should* be interested," he breathed, "because this fable's about a woman who wouldn't listen to warning."

Her heart hammering, she looked up into eyes so perilously dark they held her pinned in place.

"Her name was Blodeuwedd," he went on, his voice lowering, laced with menace. "And she was irresistible to men."

He released her wrist, and she took a startled, jerky step back, but couldn't go any farther. His eyes were hypnotic, his voice breathtakingly sensual.

"Perfection," he was saying, a cynical grate to the words. "A woman made of flowers...oak, meadowsweet and broom. She should have been Gwydion's finest creation. But he'd made a fatal mistake. He'd forgotten to ask himself one question: Where is the heart of a woman made of flowers?"

"Gwydion?"

"A wizard, a master enchanter." With cold irony, he added, "The name, Gwydion, means 'to speak poetry.' His words were said to hold sway over the things of the world."

Inexplicably Chloe's heart rate began to climb. "And the fatal mistake?"

His gaze touched hers then, connecting with an almost physical impact. After a moment it drifted to her breasts. "With all that loveliness and no heart, his creation, Blodeuwedd, became a temptress. She took the soul of every man who knew her."

A strange and irresistible sensation moved through Chloe, a quiver of near-pleasure drawn up by his eyes. "And Gwydion?" she asked faintly. "His soul, too?"

"Undoubtedly...if he'd had a soul to lose." The darkness whispered through his features again. "But Gwydion resisted. He was fated to resist. *He had to stop her.*"

How? her mind asked.

"A master enchanter and a temptress," he said as though she'd spoken. "Can you imagine what Gwydion did?" Mercifully then, his gaze moved to the ocean, releasing her. "It should have been simple enough. He created her; he could solve the problem by destroying her."

"And did he—" Anxiety closed off her throat. Why was she letting him tell her this? Why was she letting him distract her from what she'd come for?

"No...he didn't destroy her." He glanced back at her, and a low, nerve-shattering timbre edged his voice. "Shall I tell you what he did do?"

The message in his eyes brought a lightning flash of sensation, a painful thrill that nearly took her breath away. "No," she said, shaking her head, averting her eyes. *"No."* Refusing to look up at him, she blurted, "I told you, I didn't come here to hear myths and poetry. I came here to talk to you about something important." She forced her head up. "Please, I have—"

He was watching her, silent and expectant.

Something made her hesitate, a cluster of doubts pushing up to the surface. In her rush to tell him everything had she overlooked the obvious? If he was Joshua—and if he *had* done something wrong—she would be a threat to him. If he wasn't, she'd be telling a stranger the Guthries' secrets. Her stepfather's hatred of notoriety had made him one of the media's favorite prey.

Cutter had moved to the shingled wall of the motel and settled up against it. "Okay, I'll bite," he said, a mild cynicism still shading his features. "Let's hear this important revelation."

She met his eyes and a full-scale war erupted inside her. Beautiful, those eyes...*as black as midnight, Joshua's eyes.*

Suddenly, she knew what she had to do. Make this good, she thought, her heart pounding.

She moistened her paper-dry lips. "I wasn't telling you the truth this morning. I'm a partner in a small consulting firm in New York. I work with writers, actually. And I wanted to talk to you about—" inhaling, she summoned her courage "—about the possibility of your attending a symposium, perhaps speaking—"

His glower returned slowly. "Symposium? Are you serious?"

Ease out of this, she told herself, gracefully if possible, and make your exit. With a light shrug, she said, "Serious? Well, yes and no—although now that I've met you I can see a conference wouldn't be your thing. And you're probably much too busy anyway."

"Much," he assured her dryly, still angled against the wall. "For starters, I've got a half a bottle of Scotch to finish."

She detected a glimmer in his eyes, more like a twinkle really, that surprised and baffled her. After their last encounter, she'd expected an explosion. Relieved, she found herself becoming increasingly aware of his casual stance, and oddly compelled...by the rip in his jeans, of all things, and his still-untucked shirttail. This man needed care, she decided suddenly. He needed a woman. The thought gave her such an unexpected tug of longing she shoved it right out of her head.

"Drinking alone?" she inquired, her voice softer than she'd intended. When he shrugged, an admission of sorts, she added under her breath, "One of the seven symptoms of alcoholism."

Cocking his head, he stared down his nose at her, almost benevolently. "Only six to go? That should keep me busy till Tuesday."

The wry smile she detected almost persuaded her to try to engage him in further conversation...the weather? Politics? His memoirs? Or maybe just a quick rundown of his whereabouts the past fourteen years? But no, she told herself firmly, she'd recovered from the near catastrophe of spilling the whole story, and that was enough progress for the moment.

With great relief she felt the streak of practicality in her nature beginning to reassert itself. The left side of her brain seemed to be swinging some weight for the first time since she'd arrived in this misty, murky place. Oh, thank God for logic. What she needed now was another way to approach this predicament, a surefire strategy.

"Well then," she said, backing away, "I shouldn't keep you from your—" she glanced down at the glass "—pursuits any longer."

She continued backing away, not quite willing to turn around and miss the next phase of the beguiling semi-smile that was beginning to curve his lips. An enigma, this man. And at the moment just about the most gorgeous enigma she'd ever seen.

Swinging an arm behind her, she grasped her own door handle and felt relief wash through her. Her door, her room, *safety*. She looked again at the broken glass, and a daring, almost provocative grin bubbled. "By the way," she said, giving the door handle a brazen little twist. "You've got a mess to clean up."

Three

—

A surefire plan," Chloe murmured, letting her head and shoulders rest against the door she'd just closed behind her. Where in the world was she going to come up with a winning strategy against Nathanial Cutter?

She began to pace, brainstorming ideas, but nothing she came up with had the element of cleverness she'd need to worm information out of a man like Cutter. An hour later she was sprawled in a dinette chair, staring at the ceiling and entertaining thoughts of thumbscrews and Chinese water torture. In the background Frank Sinatra crooned "My Way" from the antique radio she'd switched on while pacing.

"Resume your post," she muttered, dragging the dinette chair to the window. At least she could keep an eye on Cutter's comings and goings while she plotted. She forced the rusty window lock free and eased the window pane up, startled by a breeze of near-tropical warmth. Sunshine? When had that happened?

Behind her, a deejay interrupted Frank to predict the sudden warm snap. "Don't like the weather?" he drawled laconically. "Wait a minute."

Chloe stared with disbelief at the azure skies outside. Not unlike my mercurial neighbor, she thought. Storm clouds one minute, impending sunshine the next.

She sank into the chair and slid down to prop her feet on the windowsill. She thought better with her feet up, something about alpha waves, or was it blood to the brain? Whatever it was, she needed all the biochemical advantages she could get.

It occurred to her that she might be taking the narrow view of this problem. Where was it written that she had to get her answers from Cutter himself? There might be interesting information to be had from the desk clerk, local merchants, the restaurant down the road—he had to eat somewhere—and why not contact Marsha? Her partner in New York could make a few pertinent telephone calls.

She pushed herself up in the chair, inspired. She'd ask Marsha to send her copies of all Cutter's work, and maybe do a little research on the side—a soft smile quirked—on a Welsh wizard named Gwydion.

And in the meantime, she thought, her confidence building, she'd do some close reconnaissance work on the target himself. Cutter might look invulnerable, but he had a weak spot . . . somewhere. Feeling pleased with herself, she shimmied lower in the chair and rested her head against the vinyl back to gaze out the window.

Balmy breezes ruffled the curtains and quieted her humming thoughts. Through lowering lashes she saw a bathing suit jog by. A white bathing suit. *His* bathing suit? She scraped her ankle trying to get her legs uncrossed and down from the windowsill. By the time she was vertical he was well down the beach. Oh Lord, she groaned inwardly. *Him*. In a bathing suit! And she'd missed it.

"Ouch," she grumbled, sitting back down to rub her ankle for a moment, then twisting around to catch her reflection in the vanity mirror. How did she look? "You will *not* follow him, Chloe Kates," she threatened the mirror's too bright, too eager image. "You tried that already, remember?"

She sank back down into the chair, her fingers beginning a series of drumrolls on her denim-covered thigh. The direct approach was simply too risky with an unknown quantity like Cutter. The man reacted to questions as though they were lobbed grenades.

Catching her lower lip between her teeth, she contemplated the secret weapons of female spies the world over and began to realize that her strategy had to include a plan for lowering his defenses long enough to gain his confidence.

A glimmer of an idea, half-formed, lurked seductively in a dark corner of her mind. Intrigued, she went after it.

Blodeuwedd, *the woman with no heart*. A shiver whispered through Chloe. Now there was a woman equal to the challenge of a man like Cutter. She'd lower his drawbridge... but how?

Glamour? Cool, luminous self-possession? Maybe even feminine wiles? Smiles, sighs, downcast eyes? Oh God, no. Chloe exhaled a soft moan and shook her head. No—she couldn't; she'd set the women's movement back thirty years. Besides, it wasn't her style.... It couldn't possibly work.... He'd never... While protesting, she found herself craning again to catch her reflection in the vanity mirror.

Her wide green eyes blinked with apprehension and something much more dangerous—the glitter of a woman challenged. Settle down, Lucretia Borgia, she warned with a tough maternal head shake.

Sobering, she regarded her image skeptically, but even as she inventoried her flaws, Cutter's words filtered through her thoughts. "She was irresistible to men . . . perfection." Tentatively, she touched her finger to her cheek, her lower lip. Had this face inspired such eloquence?

Her senses quickened. If he really saw her that way, then how did she use this bit of leverage to her advantage? Nothing so obvious, or dangerous, as fluttery eyelashes, of course. She might as well dangle stew meat in front of a wolf.

But cool? And luminosity? The cachet that said available, yes, but darn hard to get. She tried out a chin tilt, a smile iced with intrigue. Never her forte to be sure, but there must be some instinct lurking in her somewhere, some subliminal understanding of body language, of eye contact, of—her breath hitched in slightly—*seduction*.

Ten minutes later she'd slipped into a jade-green sundress and brushed some of the wilder kinks out of her hair. One last glance in the mirror told her she looked passably cool. Recklessly, she shrugged a camisole strap off her shoulder. "Dress for success," she murmured, heading for the door.

It took her nearly a half hour to stroll down the beach to the pier. The demands of carrying off a new image and practicing an expression of artless surprise should she run into Cutter precluded walking at a good clip.

But she didn't run into Cutter. Not a sign of him or his white trunks. Standing on the pier, she scanned the beach, hands on her hips, wondering if he might have doubled back and gone the other way toward the rocks.

The force of her disappointment surprised her. Ignoring the tightness in her chest, she started back, her mood darkening. Had he gone out of his way to avoid her? Possibilities burgeoned. Was this some kind of ruse to confuse her, to scatter her forces? Had even the Welsh-fable business been an elaborate performance staged to scare her off?

She was on her way back, only a couple of minutes from the pier, when an idea snapped her around to squint determinedly at its rickety substructure. A tiny speck dangling from a crossbeam caught her attention. Was it? She began to walk toward the pier, then to trot.

Yes, *his sunglasses*. A plan formulating, she grabbed a handful of her skirt and began to jog. Cutter had wanted those glasses back bad enough to risk life and limb for them. If she had them in her possession . . .

Each step added fresh resolve. "Mr. Cutter," she promised softly, her bare feet scattering wakes of powdery sand, "you haven't seen the last, or the best, of me yet."

Nat Cutter sat with his back and shoulders resting against the granite, his face turned to the sun, letting its warmth dry the rivulets of water that leaked from his still-wet hair. A hard run and an icy swim in the Atlantic was one sure way to work the alcohol out of his system.

And now that he was sober, he had no valid reason not to work on the story idea his publisher had been pressuring him for. Drawing up his legs, he propped a notepad on his knees and pulled off the cap of a Scripto with his teeth.

He jotted down some words, playing with a variation of a 1970s hit song. He underlined the phrase, considered it, and then began to rearrange the words. Might make a title, he thought, only mildly interested.

Other ideas came to mind, but nothing cohesive, nothing solid. So what else was new? He didn't have a story, nothing worth writing. Hadn't in years. It hadn't stopped him from churning them out though, had it? Each book more violent and sensational than the last—garbage he damn near hated. He couldn't figure how anybody else could stomach it either, but they did—his fans. They bought all his books, every one of them, and figured with each book they owned a larger chunk of his soul.

Exhaling, he shook off the mood and drew a hard horizontal slash through the words he'd written. Maybe he'd put too much of himself into those books, his own black moods.

Idly, he began to doodle. Two parallel lines and a circle and he had . . . what? A funnel, a drainpipe? Or the greased pole to oblivion, he thought ironically. A couple more circles, diagonals and ellipses and he'd created the futuristic chassis of a streamlined car.

An oval, several small graceful curves and he had the delicate workings of a woman's face. . . . God, *her* face, he acknowledged silently as he went on, adding detail as though her features were controlling the pen, his hand.

His heart began to pound harder and his hand was less steady as he worked a little faster, stroking in a lush, spiky fan of lashes over sea-green eyes. A small smile lifted the tipped-down edges of her mouth. . . .

What in the hell? he thought, staring at the image. Who was this green-eyed woman-child materializing beneath his fingers? Effortlessly, he sketched in her body, pulled back to study the effect . . . and felt a flash of desire in his groin. She looked like a mermaid shimmering out of the depths come to haunt the land . . . and its men.

His jaw flexed as he remembered her scent, her taste, so sweet it made him dizzy. Huge eyes, almost too wide-set, full of naked emotions. . . . Sobering, he recalled the hurt and bewilderment he'd seen in those eyes when he'd turned on her. God, what a ruthless bastard he could be. He knew himself to be a dangerous man, a taker, a destroyer of hope…but she'd almost made him want to feel it all again, the wonder.

He shook his head and grimaced. *What is all this drivel, Cutter? You're sounding like a man who's been without* way *too long*. Smiling grimly, he thought, *take the cure—get thee to a woman*.

His pen began to trace the line of her lower lip, shading its fullness. *But not this one… not this one*.

The aching in his gut flared, and his jaw tightened. Who was she? Why all the questions? The probing about his name? He wrote two words: *temptation, opportunity*. Circling one of them, he stared pensively at the sketch he'd brought to life and another question formed. Why was she here? *Now?*

With the pair of silver-framed Carreras tucked securely in her canvas shoulder bag, Chloe walked briskly through the fading light of dusk toward the small, two-room house that served as an office for the Sunrise motel. She breezed through the opened door and smiled at the elderly desk clerk.

Brows twitching above sharp old eyes, the senior citizen peered over his glasses and then continued reading his paper.

"Good afternoon," Chloe ventured, ignoring his what's-good-about-it expression. She brushed at the skirt of her sundress, her smile becoming more determined with each silent second. "I have something that belongs to one of the guests. He's been gone, all afternoon actually, and I thought—well, I hoped you might have some idea where I could find him."

The clerk remained serenely disinterested.

"It's Mr. Cutter," she said finally, keeping her voice low but distinct, "Nathanial Cutter?"

He blinked then. A sign of recognition, Chloe wondered, or was she being too optimistic?

Frustrated by the man's complete absorption with his paper, she began to speak faster. "I thought perhaps he might have stopped in to get his messages, maybe even mentioned where he was going. It's important that I find him, urgent actually, so if you'd be good enough to—" Her hushed entreaty flicked off like a light switch as the desk clerk regarded her askance, then folded the paper and peered up at her.

"Something you want?" He cupped a hand to his ear. "Hmm? Speak up."

He hadn't heard a word she'd said? Chloe took a breath and projected, "Nathanial Cutter," then cringed as the room became an echo chamber, seeming to ricochet her request off every wall. She looked behind her and found, to her great relief, that she and the clerk were still alone. "I'm trying to locate him."

The man shook his head and went back to his paper. "Can't help ya."

She'd prepared for that answer. "In that case I'd like to leave a message for him."

"Not much point."

"Why not? Surely he picks up his messages?"

"Might, if he had a message to pick up, but he don't. Likely never will. He ain't here."

It took her a moment to follow his logic. When she did, her pulse jumped. "He's checked out?"

"Never checked in. No one by that name staying here."

A blessedly quick idea occurred to her. If Nathanial Cutter was a pseudonym, he might have registered under his real name. "May I see your registration book?" she asked.

The clerk regarded her as one might a fly in a bakery case. "Nope." He jerked the paper high, summarily blotting her from his existence.

Taking advantage of the cover the newspaper provided, Chloe rose on tiptoe and leaned well over the walnut counter to peek at the book. It was nearly blank. There were only two names and dates: hers and—she stretched farther—the other one looked suspiciously like—

The newspaper came down with a crunch. Chloe's head snapped up so fast she was sure she'd flirted with whiplash.

"You still here?" he accused, lips pursed.

"Just leaving," she assured him, easing off the counter with a wan smile. *One inch more and she'd have read that name.*

The clerk flicked his paper meaningfully and continued reading.

She rubbed her neck and deliberated. Had this grandfatherly man just lied to her? She'd bet money he had, but why? Her curiosity piqued, she cooked up another question to stall for time. "Excuse me, but the weather's taken such a beautiful turn, I thought I'd get a little sun tomorrow."

His raised eyebrow signaled he was listening.

"And I was wondering—where would you suggest I go to do some sunbathing?"

It seemed such a harmless question she was startled when he looked up and hissed, "Stay away from those rocks down south." His eyes flashed like tiny warning strobes. "Tides are real dangerous there."

"Okay," she agreed quickly, nodding. "Thanks." Still under his scrutiny, she backed through the door, turned and started for her room. What was going on? Why the sudden outburst from a man who, from all indications, had probably read his paper through the last hurricane? Her mind began to whir. Had she unintentionally hit on something?

As she crossed the parking lot and rounded the corner of the motel, she paused to study the magnificent natural outcroppings of rock that stretched southward in a jagged, almost cruel silhouette against the skyline. A sudden chill tingled across her shoulder blades. Whatever reason the desk clerk had for warning her against that area, she was sure it had nothing to do with the tides.

Despite the fear knotting in her stomach, she instantly revised her plans. "I'll find out tomorrow," she whispered, staring at the rocks' dark hoary beauty.

The horizon was flushed with the soft promise of morning when Chloe awoke. She readied herself quickly, slipping on shorts and a halter top and collecting all the paraphernalia of a bona fide sunbather—oversized beach towel, a paperback mystery, and *his* sunglasses.

Easing open the door, she looked up and down the motel walkway and scanned the beach area quickly. She wanted the element of surprise on her side, and that meant getting to those rocks unseen. If, as she suspected, Cutter used the area for some secluded sunning or writing, she wanted to be there, pleasantly surprised, when he showed up.

Pleasantly surprised, Chloe, she reminded herself several times during her brisk walk down the beach. In the dead of the night she'd awakened with an idea, a stunningly simple way to trick him into revealing himself. The cold-bloodedness of her deception had bothered her, kept her up most of the night, in fact, seeking alternatives... until she realized that in her case the end justified the means. She had reason.

And, in truth, the ethics of deception were the least of her worries this morning. It was carrying her idea off that had her concerned. If it was to work she had to keep her wits about her, stay cool, intrigue him. Once he'd taken the bait—she shivered involuntarily—she'd spring her trap.

A sparkle in the air invigorated Chloe as she continued down the beach. The water, as slick as sheet glass, looked almost walkable, and the wraparound sky stretched so clear, so vibrantly blue that it hurt her eyes. The coming of summer to New England, she mused, breathing in deeply. Even the breeze smelled wonderful, clean and warm, laced with sunshine.

Bathed in daylight, the rocks had lost much of their menace of the night before. Their craggy peaks loomed so magically that by the time she reached them she felt almost giddily optimistic. Yesterday's dank confusion was gone, burned off by a resolute sun and a determined woman. Nat Cutter was a male. She was a female. Once again nature had come through with the basics. Now all she had to do was maximize their potential.

Whistling, she explored the jutting rocks and natural caves for the better part of an hour before her spirits began to wane. She'd expected to find something—a scrap of paper, a forgotten pencil—some clue that he'd been sequestering himself in one of the crannies she'd found.

Discouraged, she settled on a sandy niche with a view of the motel and its stretch of beach to the north. "Patience," she murmured, spreading out her towel. "Didn't somebody once predict that if you stayed in one place long enough the whole world would pass by?"

Twenty-seven sea gulls passed by in the next hour, but the rest of the world stayed put. On the twenty-eighth sea gull, Chloe had a flash of insight. *She'd been duped.* That diabolical little man had sent her off on a wild-goose chase. Lord, reverse psychology. He'd told her to stay away from the rocks knowing that's exactly where she'd go!

She planted a fist in the sand. He and Cutter were undoubtedly in cahoots, probably having a good chuckle at this very moment. Were they now planning where to send her tomorrow?

She swallowed the blasphemy that came to mind. Her outrage knew no bounds, but she wasn't about to let him rattle her again! She'd deal with this rationally even if it meant permanently clenched teeth.

Taking a deep breath, she began a calm assessment of her situation and decided that living well would have to be the best revenge for now. She'd simply stretch out, get herself a good tan and stroll back to the motel as if that's exactly what she'd intended to do all along. She'd be cool, serene, and no one would be the wiser.

She checked her hair to make sure the Carreras were secured in her curls, then lay back, arranged herself on the beach towel and offered her body to the New England sun. She'd be ready for him next time, a veritable bronzed goddess.

Closing her eyes, she envisioned herself strolling right up to him, casually flicking off the sunglasses, and with a silvery laugh, saying...what would she say? "Did you lose something, Mr. Cutter?" Well, she'd think of something devastating. She'd be silky, irresistible—she'd have it all.

Amusing herself with mental snapshots of Cutter's astonishment, she drifted off. "There's something different about you, Chloe," he'd say, visibly awed, "elusive and exciting, something I never noticed before... *Your nose is red.*"

"Nose?" she mumbled.

And then he said it again. "Your nose is red."

Her eyes popped open. Nothing. She stared straight up into azure skies. Was she having auditory hallucinations?

"Better get some sunblock on that fair skin," came the next terse observation.

She jackknifed to a sitting position. He stood at the base of the rocks, no more than six feet away. Her heart soared like a plane at takeoff. Oh God, not now, not yet. She wasn't ready to deal with him yet.

He didn't move, and some instinct told her that he was unsure, too. But he didn't look unsure. He had the white trunks on and he looked—she managed a faint-hearted swallow—magnificent.

His gaze brushed over her shorts and halter top, and she felt the irresistible evidence of male interest.

"You do have a knack for showing up in the strangest places," he muttered softly.

Pleasantly surprised, Chloe, she urged desperately. "Call it a gift," she murmured.

"There are lots of things I could call it." Irony settled in his features as his gaze flickered over the small, secluded area and finally paused on her. "Gift isn't one of them. Are you by any chance aware that this was my last bastion of privacy?"

"Really?"

"I'm curious." A dark eyebrow slanted. "How did you know I'd be here?"

He assumed she'd— Her stomach tightened. What monumental ego! That he'd assumed right was beside the point. "These rocks looked like the perfect place to sunbathe." She flashed him a smile as cool as iced tea. *"Undisturbed."*

"They are," he agreed. "Only they're my perfect place."

"Your place?"

Nodding, he moved toward her. *"Mine."*

She jerked in her legs as he neared. "No way! I got here first—*finders keepers.*" Oh Lord, had she really said that? Third-grade playground warfare lingo?

"Finders keepers?" He hesitated near her feet, a wry smile forming. "Where'd you pick up the tough talk? Harvard?"

Harvard? And then she remembered. She'd worn the garage sale T-shirt the day before.

The way he was studying her told her he wanted her to go on, to say something more. This time she knew better.

After a moment he settled his weight on one leg and folded his arms. "Looks like you and I have something in common," he acknowledged, punctuating the admission with a self-deprecatory laugh. "I don't usually admit it, but I'm an ex-Harvard reprobate, too."

"Oh?" Startled that he'd volunteered the information, she found herself smiling and nodding.

In the brief silence that followed her heart began to stir. Something in his eyes belied the quiet cynicism of his words. A softly tempered nostalgia, she realized, as he queried, "What year?"

Oh, God, what tangled webs we weave, she anguished silently as she mumbled the year she graduated NYU. So what if I didn't go to Harvard, she argued with her conscience. He thinks I did, and it's got him *interested*. What are a couple of white lies for the cause?

"A good year for redheads," he murmured.

She tried to sustain a smile, but a vague uneasiness stirred through her, hovering just out of reach, like a thought trying to resolve itself.

"Listen, about yesterday," he said, raising a shoulder, "sometimes I forget how the civilized world lives...."

She lost track of his words, lost them completely as a whisper from the past filled her mind. *Sara's run off to be with her young man from college.*

Chloe's thoughts recoiled as though she'd been struck. Nathanial Cutter had gone to Harvard—but Sara'd gone to

Elmhurst in Illinois. Her heart began to throb. Either this man was lying . . . *or he wasn't Joshua.*

She felt the blood drain from her face. Her head jerked up and her eyes fixed on Cutter as though he might instantly disappear.

"What is it?" he asked. "What's wrong?"

"Nothing," she breathed, trying desperately to conceal the emotion that trembled through her. Her head spun with confusion, ached with exploding questions, but out of the chaos one thing was clear. She'd wanted him to be Joshua. *She'd wanted every man she'd ever met to be Joshua.*

"You're white as a sheet," he said, starting toward her.

Maybe the man at the bridge had nothing to do with Sara, she reasoned urgently, maybe he'd come there for some other reason altogether. What did she really know of the Guthries? They'd been so secretive. And she'd only been at Northpointe two years.

"Chloe."

Her head came up sharply. "I'm all right," she said, her voice whisper thin. "It's just that I—" Averting her eyes, she got out, "I haven't eaten today, and I felt light-headed for a minute. But I'm fine now, really," she insisted.

Crouching, he scanned her face. "Are you sure?"

She nodded, shoring up her strength and wishing he'd stop looking at her so intently. Her heart didn't work right when he looked at her that way. You can't afford to let him stop talking now, she told herself, *not now.* "I don't think I remember you . . . in my class," she said, tilting her head, feigning mild skepticism.

His smile was fleeting. "Probably because I graduated a decade before you."

She was nodding again, wanting to believe him and still wondering why he'd brought up Harvard at all. A way of apologizing, of sharing a mutual experience?

As she glanced at him now, her heart responded to his melancholy, to the need she sensed in him. But her mind dragged up another terrible possibility. Was he intentionally leading her astray? Was he feeding her lies to throw her off the track? Even at the thought she felt a soft ache in her chest. Keep going, keep him talking, she told herself. "You were an English major?" she asked.

He nodded. "Yeah, you?"

Before she could answer, a grin transformed his features; a smile so boyish, so vulnerable that she felt a tug at her heart.

"Evans Cole," he murmured. "God, the holy terror of the English department. Was he still teaching when you were there? Did you take his Critical Analysis class?"

His openness was disarming... but hadn't he caught her just this way before—with a trick question? Please God, she thought, don't let this be another one. Smiling, she pretended to remember. "Quite a guy, Evans Cole."

"A wild man," he agreed, laughing. "Used to squint at us through those Coke-bottle glasses. 'Furor scribendi,' he'd rant, 'none of you has the rage to write!' "

His laughter was so low and rich, so genuine she found herself smiling with him... and sobering instantly as he turned to her. "What do you think," he asked, his voice lowering to a husky whisper, his features gradually shading with that breathtaking darkness, "was George Sand right? Are those of us who don't remember the past condemned to relive it?"

As the words registered, her body convulsed with a soft, audible gasp. "What do you mean?"

But he was already looking away at the water, traces of an inner conflict working in his features. "Nothing," he said finally. "I didn't mean anything." Rising, he walked to the water, his back to her.

"I'm keeping you from your sunbathing, boring you with war stories," he said. "I don't know why the hell I brought up Harvard anyway. Some of us never do grasp the social graces." As he turned, his eyes met hers briefly, but with such a burst of intensity she lost a heartbeat. "Once a selfish SOB," he vowed quietly, "always a selfish SOB."

It sounded like a warning. Still, she couldn't help herself. "Wait," she said as he started away.

His head came around.

"I love war stories." She smiled wistfully, foolishly, her heart thumping. "Anyway, what's the hurry?" Color seeped into her cheeks. "We don't have to talk about Harvard if you'd rather not. I didn't find the place all that memorable either."

The conflict in his eyes intensified, and one message came pulsing through. Unless she was wrong, he wanted to stay with her. "You came for some sun," she added softly, "and this is your bastion, after all."

Was he turning back? "There's plenty of room," she pressed shamelessly. "I'll share."

His eyes grazed her face, lingering on her mouth for a second before returning to her eyes. "Sorry, I never learned to share. A selfish SOB, remember?"

Startled, she watched him turn and walk away.

It was an instant before she realized she was springing to her feet, calling after him, "You're right, Cutter. You are devoid of social graces." A flush stained her cheeks. "Can we chalk this one up to bad manners, too? Or is it *me* that brings out the worst in you?"

He was slowing. *He stopped.*

Her heart thudded as he turned around. Fighting off tremors of apprehension, she began to walk toward him. "I don't think you're nearly as socially retarded as you pretend," she said. "It's me, isn't it? I think I threaten you. Is that it? Do I threaten you, Mr. Cutter?"

She saw him stiffen, felt her nervous system jump in response. She took two more steps, a deliberate challenge, and held her ground. God, but he frightened her.

His eyes began to glitter, lit from some terrifying inner source. "Yes," he said, taking his time as he closed the distance between them. "I suppose you do threaten me."

She tried to look away as he neared, but she couldn't. "I knew it," she breathed. "Why?"

He hesitated imperceptibly, inches from her. "Because you want something from me."

"No—" she started.

He moved in tight then, flush with her body, the implicit threat stunning her to silence. A liquid weakness assailed her legs, a flowing of sensation that bled away her strength in one climbing jolt. "No," she whispered, trying to step back, desperate to free herself from the energy shimmering around her like a live electrical field.

"I don't know what you're after," he said, his voice resonating through her mind, "but be careful. I stopped giving people what they wanted years ago."

His features were angry, his eyes dark, but she felt a soft shimmer along the line of her throat. His fingertips . . . and they trembled slightly as they touched her.

Thoughts rippled through her mind, her body—thoughts that couldn't be her own. *I don't want much,* a voice was whispering inside her, *not much . . . just his soul.*

"What did you say?" No longer gentle, his voice was harsh, commanding.

Nothing, she tried to tell him, but she could only shake her head . . . and watch the tumult building in his eyes. Vaguely aware of a pressure lifting, she realized his hand was gone from the column of her throat.

"Why are you here?" he exhaled, shifting back. "Why the hell aren't you running the other way?"

A flush of color warmed her face and inexplicably, almost recklessly, her nerve came tumbling back. "I never was any good at track," she declared softly. At his grimace, she pulled a breath, steeling herself. "I'm not going anywhere, Cutter. I'll stay and take my chances."

She saw immediately that she'd made a tactical error. He'd taken it as a challenge. Catching her arm, he urged her closer, his breath cooling the dampness at her temples. "How much of a gambler have we got here?"

Her heart began to thump erratically. He's teasing, she told herself, trying to frighten me. "I guess that depends on what I want, doesn't it?"

"And you're not going to tell me, are you?" His eyes glinted. "Yesterday I was wondering about the difference between temptation and opportunity. Today, I know. You, redhead, are temptation." The muscles in his hand flexed and contracted around her arm; his eyes burned with a light that made her shiver. "And that," he grated softly, "makes me vulnerable to you."

She met his eyes and felt a shock of awareness. "It does?" The implications of this windfall took her breath away. And after a moment so did its obvious drawbacks. "And you're not a man who likes to feel vulnerable."

"Hate it," he admitted, releasing her arm to brush a stray tendril of hair from her cheek. His features moved with the darkness that made her forget how to breathe. "But I can't resist temptation."

His lips parted slightly, an almost irresistible moistness to them, and her stomach clutched in anticipation. Closing her eyes, she felt a sharp ache in the back of her throat as she remembered the sweetness of his mouth.

"God, you are dangerous," he breathed.

A sensation was unfurling inside her, the soft swirl of pain that comes with needing something so badly you ache for it. *Touch me,* she heard the voice inside her whispering to him, the words repeating until they filled her like the shivering cry of tiny bells. *I need you to touch me.*

She gasped as she felt his hands sliding up her shoulders to rest at the curve of her neck. As his fingers spread, enclosing her throat, she surrendered to the sweet riot of emotion inside her.

He bent to take her lips, his whispering darkness moving over her, hesitating, and then his mouth touched hers with a tiny, almost audible cry of sensation.

Her inner world dissolved into chaos and went pale with light, the flash of a tiny, soundless explosion. It was beautiful, endless. And all she could remember next was being gathered up in the hard crush of his arms, absorbed into him until she only existed through the tender, frenzied brushings of his mouth.

She felt him shudder, heard his ragged breathing, and a flushed scent filled her nostrils—heat, the heat of a climbing fever.

A sound rumbled in his chest, the sensual rattling of an animal's growl. Working his hands into her hair, coiling, no longer gentle, he suddenly broke the kiss. "Chloe," he warned, his voice broken, searingly harsh, "don't do this."

With a convulsive tremor, he lifted his head, his eyes shut. "God bless it, *don't do this to me.*" Just a breath away from her lips, a pulse throbbed in his neck.

"What?" she whispered, her fingertips at his jawline.

"Damn," he rasped softly, "I knew this would happen." Looking down at her, anger and frustration high in his eyes, he said, "You're killing me, you know that? Killing me by inches, ripping my willpower to shreds." His long,

rough exhalation bathed her face. "I want to see you again, no—I *have* to see you again...tonight?"

"Tonight?" she echoed, dazed. "Like a...do you mean...a date?"

"Oh God," he groaned, shaking his head, "yes, a date—if that's what you want, a date."

He pulled back, releasing her, still shaking his head. "Turn me down," he exhaled. "Say no while you can."

"Never."

"Okay," he said, gazing at her with such intensity she felt weak, "but don't say I didn't warn you." He turned away and began to jog toward the motel.

"What time?" she called after him.

"Seven," he yelled over his shoulder.

"Seven," she murmured, a shaky grin tugging at her lips. "I'll have to check my calendar."

Four

Chloe hadn't prepared for a date with such frenetic energy since the sophomore prom. Success *was* sweet, she decided, poring over her limited wardrobe. But fleeting. Her blissful smile turned practical. She had to look good tonight—irresistible, if she could swing it. She finally opted for a white eyelet sundress with an old-fashioned lace-up bodice.

One look in the mirror and she didn't need any blusher. Her small breasts were buoyed up, full and blooming, by the gentle supports of the white cotton bodice. The nipped-in waist and swirling ruffled skirt further sensualized her petite figure. And her hair, freshly shampooed and brushed at length to loosen the curl, swirled around her shoulders like the mane of a glossy, red-gold animal. Green eyes shimmered against tawny, sunbrushed skin, and a touch of powder quieted the dappling of freckles that decorated the narrow bridge of her nose.

"Chloe," she whispered, stunned at the effect. "He's a goner. The woman you see before you is living proof of the miracle of modern cosmetology. One bat of these Fabulashes, and he'll give away the farm!"

A faint tap at the door made her stiffen nervously. She glanced at the clock. Six-fifteen? He was forty-five minutes early. "He must be even more anxious than I am," she realized with hushed surprise.

She reached for the doorknob gingerly, eased the door open and registered the blink of huge faded blue eyes beneath thick wire-rimmed glasses. The desk clerk.

Her unexpected visitor looked as surprised as she felt. "Did you want something?" she asked.

"Nope," he said, clipping the word off even more closely than usual.

"You didn't?" She blinked. "But you knocked."

He shook his head and held up a well-worn broom. "Sweepin' the walk. Mighta bumped your door by mistake." With a surprisingly polite nod, he added, "Sorry."

Suspicion prickled in Chloe's brain. Much too chummy. Was he trying to smile his way out of something? Like...listening at her door, perhaps?

She glanced toward Cutter's room and saw the clerk following her gaze. Their eyes flicked back and locked for an instant.

With a twitch of self-consciousness, the clerk looked off at the horizon. "Gonna be a warm one," he said, speaking apparently of the impending evening.

Down the beach a flock of gulls swooped and darted in a raucous display of daredeviltry.

"Umm," Chloe conceded, trying to decide whether or not to tell him she had a date with his missing motel guest, Nathanial Cutter. As he wandered away, whistling tunelessly and sweeping, she called out, "By the way—"

His wise-old-owl expression as she turned back made her hesitate.

"How long you staying?" he asked, out of the blue, his head tilted down, his eyes dead level, very much the judge asking the defendant, "How do you plead?"

"I don't know." The halting inflection in her voice made her add defensively, "Does it matter?"

"Might," he said, "might not."

She refused to acknowledge the cold tickle of anxiety in her stomach. "What does that mean?"

"Means you been here longer than most already." He hiked the broom up under his arm, holding it horizontal, the handle end pointed at her like a shotgun barrel.

"Three days is longer than most?" She tried to smile. "Must be difficult to make a living with such a turnover."

"Living," he muttered obliquely, "ain't difficult if a body uses the sense God gave him." His eyes drifted south, beyond her, toward the rocks. "Now animals, they got sense. Hunted animals got an instinct. Something tells 'em when to run, when to hold still. Humans, they've lost it. Most of 'em don't even know they're being stalked." Without moving his head, just his eyes, he looked at her. "Easy targets, humans, fish in a barrel."

He wheeled around, made his slow-gaited, deliberate way to the end of the walkway and disappeared around the side of the building.

Chloe closed her eyes in frustration. The tickle of anxiety was now a soft throb. *He'd frightened her again.* That strange little man could frighten a rock!

In the next forty minutes, she successfully convinced herself that she had a latent talent for turning slightly morbid senior citizens into Alfred Hitchcock characters. He's probably alone too much, she decided. A golden-agers club would do him wonders.

She forced her mind to dwell on bigger and better things. It was five to seven and she had the evening of her life ahead of her. Where would "tall, dark and handsome" take her tonight? Dinner? Dancing? Anticipation expanded in her chest like a bubble. *Would she find out who he was tonight?* The fact that he'd admitted his vulnerability to her, even given in to it for a moment, gave her a measure of confidence, perhaps more than she deserved to feel. Were tamed wolves ever safe? Weren't they known to turn feral unexpectedly—and usually just when their human captor succumbed to overconfidence? Or that other human failing, trust?

By seven-ten, her confidence was already on the wane.

At seven-thirty, she heard footsteps and rushed to the door, her hand poised on the doorknob. Let him knock first, then count to ten, she cautioned. He's thirty minutes late; he can darn well wait thirty seconds more. And *please*, Chloe, stay cool, unruffled. Think luminous.

She kicked off her shoes, a last-minute inspiration. Oh, was he late? Really? She hadn't noticed. She wasn't quite ready, either.

The tap was so faint she barely heard it. She pulled the door open and searched empty air. It took her longer than it should have to realize she hadn't heard a knock. There hadn't been one.

With creeping chagrin, she stepped outside her door and looked down at his, afraid any minute he'd come out and catch her craning her neck like a ninny. He wants to look good and he's taking extra time to get ready, she decided. That's why he's late.

By eight o'clock, she'd flattened herself against the thin wall that connected their rooms, listening, hearing nothing. An hour late? What was he doing? No one needed to look that good. Should she casually wander over? No, she'd wait him out. This was obviously a test. He wanted to be *pursued*!

By nine she'd run out of excuses for him. The Carreras she'd forgotten to return that afternoon were staring at her from the bureau top. Pretty flimsy, she realized, but better than no reason at all.

Sunglasses in hand, she approached his room and hesitated. The dark windows signaled her that something was wrong.

Her knock went unanswered. She knocked louder, then again. Nothing.

He'd gone, she realized, stepping back from the door. It came upon her all at once, the stunned disappointment, like an accidental elbow to the ribs. Halting, sighing softly, she said it aloud, "He's gone," and the whispered statement made it irrefutably true. He'd stood her up, *run out on her.*

She didn't know how long she stood there, staring at the darkened room before she began to back away. A soft aching filled her throat as she turned and hurried back to her own room.

The plastic wall clock above the dinette told Chloe she'd been sitting, staring at a crack in the flowered wallpaper and listening to the old radio play mood music for more than an hour. She hadn't even changed her dress.

She glanced around, noticed the Carreras on the tabletop where she'd tossed them. "I hate those glasses," she whispered suddenly, a catch in her voice. "Almost as much as their owner."

A small flame burned near her heart. Never in her life had she felt so many emotions in the course of an hour: piercing disappointment, and then hurt out of all proportion to her predicament. And finally, the soft ache in her throat had tightened into a knot that was hard to swallow over. Now she was angry. *I know nothing about him—and that probably includes his name—and still I care enough to want to hate him for running out on me,* she thought, furious. *How did he do that? Make me care? I hate him for that.*

She came out of the chair, pacing randomly, changing directions like a broken compass needle. Yes, she was angry, and she wanted to be angrier, because the flame hadn't yet burned all the hurt from her heart; the blue mists of disappointment weren't completely dissipated.

"Pull yourself together," she muttered under her breath, not because she meant it, but because after her emotional roller coaster of an hour some gesture of self-control seemed called for. "You've been stood up before."

It took awhile, but the words finally worked. Gradually almost in spite of herself, she felt the emotions giving way to a kind of detachment. Go to bed, get some sleep, she told herself, but vague stirrings of purpose kept her pacing. By the time she'd undone her bodice ties and left her dress in a heap on the floor, a clear, almost ruthless sense of direction had cut through her turmoil.

Okay, Cutter, she thought, if this is how you want to play, you're on. You want to play games, I can play games. You want to play hardball, I can play hardball.

Riffling through her suitcase for her nightgown, she came upon the two tiny bottles of vodka that she'd purchased on the plane flight, thinking she'd need sedation. It wasn't sedation she needed now, but somehow a belt of booze seemed like the right gesture, considering her mood.

"Hard liquor, hardball and a hard-hearted woman," she said, a dry smile tightening her lips. It felt good not to care. It felt even better knowing she was damn well going to get what she came here for. Answers. She wouldn't leave this place until she knew whether or not he was Joshua. And Sara, she thought resolutely, pulling out her nightgown and slipping it over her head. One way or another, she intended to find out what had happened to her stepsister.

Gritting her teeth, she gripped one of the little bottles firmly, unscrewed the cap and took a swig. With a choking sound she swallowed it, then gasped for air as it seared her throat and stung her eyes. She'd forgotten how thoroughly she disliked the taste of alcohol. Stubbornly, she took another drink.

Not bothering to pull down the quilt, she sank onto the bed, propped herself up with pillows and finished the bottle. First thing in the morning she'd start with the desk clerk. A shakedown, she thought, savoring the words. That little bugger knew plenty, and if he wouldn't cough it up, she'd—

When nothing came immediately to mind, she opened the second bottle, took a drink, and decided the taste had possibilities. Sort of warm and sweet, like mouthwash. Maybe she'd offer the clerk money. Everybody had a price.

Everyone but *him*, her fuzzying mind declared.

Settling down into the pillows, her eyelids drooping a little, she decided to case the area once she'd finished with the desk clerk. Someone must know Cutter. And where were those books Marsha was supposed to send her? And that mini-investigation her partner had promised to run on Cutter? She'd call New York first thing in the morning.

The next inspiration swept into her mind from out of nowhere. *She could search his room.* There had to be clues among his personal things, mementos, letters. An address book? A personal journal?

Like a stop-action photograph, her eyes blinked open by degrees. *Break* into his room? She was scheming like a seasoned sociopath. Focusing in on the half-empty bottle she was clutching, she decided it must be the alcohol talking. She relegated the vodka to the bedside table and switched out the light.

Rolling over, she curled up and burrowed into the quilt as she drew it over herself. Grateful for the liquor's soporific effect, she heard herself murmuring, "He'll never know what hit him," as she drifted into sleep.

Wrenching up, still dazed with sleep, Chloe listened, all her senses alerted. What had awakened her?

She scanned the room, searching its corners, seeing wraiths in each flickering shadow. The stillness assured her that no one was there . . . but something had awakened her.

Sounds. She heard them again.

A muffled noise came from somewhere. And again.

The bedside clock said 3:00 a.m. Twisting around in the direction of Cutter's room, she listened. Voices, muted but somehow strained, indistinguishable words, the bang of something dropped . . . or thrown? Someone was there.

Him? He's back! Leaping from the bed, she stumbled through the darkness to the wall and pressed herself against it. He was talking—no, arguing—with someone.

She strained to hear the other voice, to make out the muffled high-pitched sounds vibrating in her ears. "No," she cried softly and stepped back. A woman, she realized, continuing to back away from the wall. *He was with a woman*.

Faltering to the bed, she sat, paralyzed with disbelief, her brain refusing to assimilate what she'd just heard.

The sounds carried through the wall again. The blurred voices of a man and woman in rapt conversation. The acrid taste of shock was rising inside Chloe, swimming in her throat. "Oh, my God," she repeated, her hand flying to her mouth.

The sounds quieted, and Chloe's head jerked up. She wanted to listen; she couldn't bear to listen. It was only as she lay back on the bed, still clutching her hand to her mouth that she experienced a wrench of awareness. *The woman with him could be Sara.*

She got up fast, the nerves in her body sparking like raw wires. Perching rigidly on the edge of the bed, she felt an upsurge of conflict. *Sara.*

Her arms and legs felt like lead as she struggled out of her nightgown and pulled on jeans and a T-shirt. She had to know—but what if it *was* her stepsister?

Joshua and Sara. The image of an intense young man and a fragile blond woman sent Chloe's thoughts hurtling back fourteen years. She knew instinctively that the truth would be more painful if the woman was Sara. Faced with the dilemma she'd suppressed all these years, Chloe's fears suddenly became clear: finding Sara meant losing Joshua.

Her throat tightened. He was never mine to lose, she told herself, he was just a lonely child's fantasy. But she knew it was more than that. Joshua was a beckoning dream she'd never been free of since the first moment she'd seen him. She shook her head. How could a dream hold such power over the human heart?

One part of her wanted to run, to avoid the pain of reality, whatever it might be. Another part of her wouldn't rest until she knew.

Sinking to the floor, she forced on her tennis shoes, her breathing shallow as she struggled back to her feet and walked to the door. She gripped the knob hard to stop her hand from shaking. "Open it," she ordered.

Outside, the still night air heightened her sense of caution as she approached his door. Confused, she slowed and halted. The room was as dark as before. At first she thought she must be going crazy, and then an odd sensation passed through her, almost relief, and she began to shake. They've left, she thought, slumping against the shingled wall for support.

As the shaking subsided another possibility occurred to her. What if he'd taken the woman, whoever she was, to bed? Chloe's heart constricted. Fighting to catch her breath, she rushed to her room, slammed the door and walked blindly across to the bed. The second bottle of vodka sat on the bedside table where she'd left it.

She drank it all, the hot stream of alcohol scoring her throat and backing up into her nasal passages. Again, the urge to run away, to escape, overtook her.

She caught hold of the bedpost and hung on until the shaking eased. All her life she'd been running from the emotional debris of her past. As a child she'd lost herself in daydreams to avoid the pain of her parents' divorce and later her mother's death. As an adult she'd lost herself in work to forget the years at Northpointe.

Staring down at the empty bottle in her hand, she realized the race was over. She could never run far enough or fast enough. The past had caught up with her.

Shivering in the early-morning dampness, Chloe walked toward the motel office. One way or the other that desk clerk was going to answer her questions this time, she resolved. This place had become her Holy Grail.

She tried the door of the motel office and found it locked. A dim halo reflected in the window caught her attention. The office itself was dark, but a vertical ribbon of light filtered through the partially opened door of the back room where the clerk lived.

She considered knocking and then discarded the idea, realizing the empty office might be an unexpected opportunity. Hardly believing what she was about to do, she searched her purse for a credit card.

The oil card buckled several times as she tried to work it into the doorjamb. It all looked so easy on television!

Expecting to be caught at any moment, she glanced through the window and then over her shoulder. "Breaking and entering," she reminded herself under her breath, "is a felony in every state in the union."

As she nursed the card in farther and angled it up, a faint click sounded and the knob gave. Her stomach knotted with anxiety.

She slipped into the office. From the next room she heard the slow-gaited shuffle of slippers on hardwood, and then a faucet creaked on and water began to pour. *Now,* she told herself, letting out a taut breath.

She moved to the counter and saw the registration book lying closed on the desk. Rising on tiptoes, she grasped for it when a shrill ring stopped her hand in midair. Her heart surged so chaotically she wasn't sure what she'd heard. And then it shrilled again. The phone.

Lunging for the book, she flipped it open, riffling pages until she found her own name. The other entry on that page, the one she'd tried to see two days before, was Nathanial Cutter.

Nearing footsteps brought her up. Scanning the room frantically, she saw a door at the far end and ran for it, slipping inside as the phone shrilled again.

Crouched in what appeared to be a storage room, she realized she'd learned little beyond the fact that the clerk had lied. *Cutter was registered*—under his own name—and the clerk had denied it. But what did that mean? Probably nothing, she reasoned through rising disappointment, other than the fact that he'd been trying to protect Cutter's privacy.

Her heart was hammering so wildly that she almost missed the name Cutter when the clerk mumbled it. Her senses alerted, she strained to pick up more of the brief conversation. One other name registered—White Rock. The rest was indistinguishable.

The instant she heard the click of the phone receiver, Chloe remembered she'd left the registration book open. Would the clerk notice it? Would he check and find the front door unlocked?

For an interminable moment there was only silence. And then the sound of footsteps receding and the creak of a faucet signaled that she was safe. Her legs threatening to give way, she crept from the office and sprinted through the patchy, low-lying mist to her room.

White Rock, she learned through a phone call to the Belmont Chamber of Commerce, was one of several small populated islands off the coast of Maine. An hour's drive would take her to the ferry landing in Belmont, and another thirty-minute boat crossing would take her to the island.

She reinforced her decision to go with a mental nod, tossed her weekender on the bed, opened it and began packing for the eventuality of an overnight stay. Not that she planned an overnight stay, but if she was on to something...

She was in the bathroom, trying to force a traveler-size tube of Colgate into an overstuffed makeup bag, when the creak of a door opening caught her attention. It was such a faint noise she thought she'd imagined it—or that it was someone else's door.

A cool breeze flowed past her ankles, a tangy whiff of ocean air. Had the wind blown the door open?

She caught the hushed sound of something moving, approaching; it pricked at her senses more than her ears. Staring at her frozen reflection in the medicine-cabinet mirror, she waited. Her knuckles white on the makeup case, she listened for footsteps.

The quiet had a paralyzing effect.

"Who's there?" she called.

Clutching her makeup case, stiff-armed, she came around and cautiously entered the living room.

The motel doorway hung wide open, filled by a gold-fringed silhouette.

Her heart jerked. *"You,"* she breathed.

His eyes purple-shadowed, his hair softly mussed, Nat Cutter assumed his favorite stance—shoulder propped against the doorframe, weight casually distributed along the diagonal line of his body.

"Am I late?" he asked quietly.

She hesitated, then realized he meant last night. *"Late?"* The word hung in the air precariously. A twitch of pain bit at her mouth. "No—I'd call it a clean miss."

"Sorry," he said, his voice so low she had to read his lips to understand him, and then he asked, "You going somewhere?"

She turned her back on him and tossed the makeup case into the weekender. "Yes," she hissed softly. With two brisk strides, she reached the bed, snapped the suitcase shut and pulled it to the floor. How *dare* he show up this way? The bastard! Leaning on her door as though he held a lease on the threshold.

"Where?" he said.

Name, rank and serial number, she told herself bitterly. The Geneva Convention required no more information than that to be given to the enemy. She came around, prepared to deliver a withering look and order him out of her doorway and her life . . . but instead she caught her foot on the weekender and tipped it over on her toes.

The pain made her face go white.

He grinned slightly. "Is this another ploy for emergency medical care?" He started toward her.

With a furious shake of her head she held him at bay. "Don't you touch me." *Don't even think about touching me.* A tear of sheer frustration rolled down her cheek. She had to get him out of here. She should hate him. *She did hate him*, enough to murder him. But not— Her stomach wrenched brutally. Not enough to stop him if he tried to—

"Hey," he said, sobering. "Does it hurt that bad?"

"Yes." Yes, it hurt that bad.

She picked up the suitcase and stared fixedly through him at the door. "I'm leaving, Cutter. Get out of my way."

"Not until you tell me where you're going."

"I'd rather die first," she muttered, her fingers tightening on the handle.

"I don't think we have to go that far," he said, his voice lowering. "But you're not leaving."

Anger flared inside her throat. And then she made the mistake of looking at him, at his features with their shadowed and conflicting needs, at his eyes as he neared, black magic, beautiful...terrible.

Five

Panic flashed through Chloe. She thrust out an arm, her palm a vertical barrier. "Stay away from me, Cutter, I mean it."

He hesitated, a question in his eyes. "I don't get it. You're leaving because of last night?"

She realized then that he thought she was returning to New York, and in her fury, she hadn't the slightest inclination to set him straight. The disquiet in his features brought a flicker of satisfaction.

"Why?" he asked, moving toward her.

"Why not?" Warning him off with her hand, she stepped back and lost her grip on the suitcase. It hit the floor with a jarring clatter, popped open and spewed out clothes and makeup everywhere.

Staring down at the hopeless mess, Chloe felt a surge of frustration out of all proportion to the situation. *"Damn,"* she moaned, fighting back the threat of tears.

Static burst from the old radio, interrupting a medley of Tony Bennett hits. Each discharge sent a tense crackle through the room.

Nat Cutter's brows furrowed in confusion as he watched Chloe struggle to repack the bag. She was muttering, throwing clothes into the suitcase and hastily wiping her cheek, but not quickly enough to hide the tears he saw quivering in her lower lashes.

Crying? "Chloe, what's—"

"I dropped my suitcase," she snapped as though that event were an unspeakable tragedy. "My clothes, they're—" The words broke off with a choked sound.

"Hey," he said, his voice gentling. "It's not the end of the world. I'll help you."

"No." Her body stiffened, her hands worked faster.

Conflict stemmed high in his chest. He'd come to tell her he was sorry, to explain about last night—why he hadn't shown up, all the reasons he couldn't see her again. He'd expected anger, but not this. She looked like a small cornered animal crouching there, full of sadness and spirit, trying for all she was worth to pull off a dignified exit.

"Chloe," he said, controlling his voice against the unexpected tightening in his chest. "Tell me what's going on."

She shook her head and fumbled to close the suitcase, shuddering when the lock snapped shut. As she rose and picked up the bag, another unexpected impulse hit him. He wanted to stop her. What the hell's wrong with you, man? he questioned, almost violently. She's leaving. She's solving the problem for you. Let her go. *It's better this way.*

But he knew he was blocking her exit. And he didn't move.

She walked to within two feet of him and came to a stiff stop, avoiding his eyes, obviously building her courage to walk around him. Drawing in a breath, he remembered the way she'd come sprinting down that dock two days before, a redheaded, one-woman rescue squad, determined to save him from himself.

Watching her now, her eyes downcast, her lashes a spiky silhouette against her pale cheeks, he felt a wrench of something alien inside him. Need. The need to kiss away the dampness that still clung to her lashes. An almost savage need to soothe her hurt and feel the softness of her mouth beneath his.

An incredible mouth, he thought, mesmerized by its vulnerability. Sensual, full…the lower lip pouting slightly when she wasn't smiling, like now.

Let her go, he told himself. She's got trouble written all over her. If you ever needed to stay clear of a woman it's this one. She's impulsive, romantic, always on the verge of something half-crazy. You know the type, man. Wide-eyed, and breathless, an infectious spirit that wants to take up residence in your soul—he felt a wrench of desire in his gut—*the kind you can't make love to and ever hope to walk away from.*

Maybe that was it, he thought, grasping at anything. Hell, yes, that was it. He wanted to get her into bed. He'd been obsessed with the thought of making love to her since he'd sketched her picture two days before.

His eyes moved over her body involuntarily, aware of the rebellious pride in her carriage. Almost as though she sensed his gaze, she stiffened her spine, and the result was a defiant arch that pulled the thin cotton fabric of her Harvard T-shirt tight over her breasts.

Before he could block it out, his memory was replaying their encounter on the beach the day before. The fine quiver that had moved through her when he touched her. Her starry-eyed sensuality as she looked up at him, as though he was the man she'd been waiting for all her life. Why had she looked at him like that? *What in the hell did she want from him, anyway?*

The sound of her throat clearing brought him back.

"Move out of the way," she said, still not looking at him.

The impulse that sparked in his muscles jarred him. Her body was rigid with determination, her will, awesome... but she was tiny compared to him, a foot smaller, easily managed. He could stop her without half trying; he could stop her, hold her— A flash of desire nearly cut off his breathing. You're losing it, he warned savagely, *get out of her way.*

"Move aside, Cutter," she insisted, her voice wire-taut as she raised her strained features to his. *"Now."*

Her mouth was soft, defiant. Let her go, he argued with his hot-blooded impulses. She's trouble, man. She's been asking questions. *She wants something.*

But it wasn't his own warning that made him step aside. It was the light in her eyes; he'd never seen such fierceness of will in a woman. This one had been through some kind of hell and survived it, he realized instantly. And whatever she was going through now, she'd survive that, too.

He gave her plenty of room, and felt the constriction in his throat as she walked past him with unsteady pride.

"Chloe," he heard himself say as she approached the open door. "Why?"

She hesitated, a shudder moving her shoulders.

In the distance, sea gulls keened, counterpoint to the soft crash of the incoming tide.

"At least tell me why you're leaving."

Poised on the threshold, Chloe felt the rasp in his voice caress her like raw silk. She gripped her suitcase so tight her knuckles stung. If she stopped now, if she even attempted to answer his question, she would never make it out the door—that was the extent of his effect on her. And he knew it. She was sure now that he knew the power he had over her even if he didn't understand it.

"If this is about last night, look, I'm sorry, I—"

A muscle spasmed in her cheek. *"Don't,"* she cut in, swinging around to face him. "Don't explain. I don't want to hear it."

"I had an emergency—"

"Emergency?" she cut him off bitterly. "Is that what they're calling it nowadays?"

His one-shouldered shrug brought her simmering hurt and fury to full boil. He dared to stand there and act perplexed? "I heard the woman, Cutter."

"You heard— When?"

"Last night," she bit out. "Late, in your room."

Stunned, he stared at her for a moment, his features slowly mobilizing with awareness, and then he began to shake his head and walk toward her. "No," he said, "you didn't hear a woman."

Incredulity left her speechless. Now he was going to tell her what she'd heard? She felt the suitcase slipping from her fingers and set it down.

"You couldn't have heard a woman," he insisted, an odd intensity in the voice. Before she could think to stop him he was standing in front of her, staring down at her, paralyzingly near. "It was something else, the television maybe." His shoulder lifted again. "I couldn't sleep last night, I had it on—"

"Television?" She pulled back, her voice taut with disbelief. "Oh Cutter, do you expect me to believe that? I heard her, I heard her."

"No." His breath fanned over her face. "It was something else, Chloe...maybe you had a dream."

His closeness was dizzying; his warm male scent permeated her senses. And when his fingers grazed down her arm she felt a fine spray of sparks that drew every cell of her attention to the hand that was closing around her wrist.

"You had a dream," he was telling her with such conviction she almost believed him. "It frightened you, woke you up. We all think we hear things in the middle of the night."

She shook her head, determined to hold out against the irresistible pull in his voice. "No, I heard you—arguing with her. I heard something drop. I—"

She broke off as he glanced at her mouth, just the way he had the day before at the beach. *Just before he'd kissed her.* Her hand flew up to cover the vulnerable area. She couldn't let him kiss her now. That would be the end of her.

Startled, he almost smiled, and then his eyes narrowed, lit with inner flickerings of regret. "Chloe," he insisted, exhaling, tugging her wrist. "I'm sorry I couldn't make our date last night. I wanted to, but I had an emergency. There wasn't time to tell you, and I got back too late to wake you."

He cradled her hand in his, and with gentle unconscious strokes of his thumb, he began to caress the icy coldness from her fingers. "I couldn't sleep so I turned on the televison. That must be what you heard."

"The television..." Looking into his eyes, she felt a dull thud of pain in her chest. Why was he lying to her?

His hand came up to cup her jawline, and she felt the slight unsteadiness in his fingers. "I wanted to be with you last night." His voice was so husky with sincerity that despite her skepticism, she wanted to close her eyes and try to capture its resonance.

"Do you believe me?" he asked.

"Yes... I believe you wanted to be with me."

She saw the slight tremor in his jaw, saw the muscle catch as he searched her features. His mouth moved, tautening sensually, and a thrill built deep inside her.

"There is no other woman, Chloe."

Staring up at him, transfixed, she nearly buckled under the eloquent and complex message filling her senses, it's meaning just beyond her grasp. *Other* woman. What did that mean? In that abrupt starburst of a moment, she had no inkling of understanding other than that he was sincere. He was trying to tell her something, and for him, it was truth.

His gaze held hers until she felt lights darting inside her, primitive messages rushing through her senses. The waver of his forefinger along her lip line sparked a run of electricity, and she reacted instantaneously, her body starting as though a live current had arched through her.

He bent toward her, breathtaking, and it happened again. Just as before when his lips had touched hers, she felt that infinitesimal jolt of sensation, the burst of light behind her eyelids. Deep inside her a warm glow fanned out like a sunrise, and then fell in on itself, gathering energy to expand in another wave of radiance.

Sweet chaos rushed up like a spring tide as he broke the kiss, his hands framing her face in a hovering caress, his thumbs at the corners of her mouth. After a moment, the muscles of his face relaxed, and a slight smile creased his lips. "Tell me the truth. Were you really going to leave?"

"No," she assured him, barely able to talk. "No, just a day trip." And then she added without thinking, "To White Rock."

His fingers contracted. "What?"

Awareness exploded in her brain. What had she done?

In the horrible moment that followed, she would have given anything to take the words back, but it was too late, she'd said it...and the conflict was already rising in his eyes.

He released her, shifting back, searching her face. "The island? What do you want there?"

"Nothing in particular," she said, the lie tangling in her throat. "I—I heard it's beautiful, a must-see for tourists. There's a ferry from Belmont." She glanced down at the suitcase. "I thought I might stay over." It sounded so lame, she couldn't imagine anyone believing it, especially him.

He stared at her for silent, stretching moments. Several times she thought he was on the verge of speaking. But he didn't. He nodded, simply nodded and turned away, his face unreadable.

She suppressed a shiver as a cold rush of ocean air chased the residual heat of his body from her skin. He looked more guarded than angry as he walked to the open doorway and stared out. Dr. Jekyll and Mr. Hyde, this man. Which one was he becoming now?

The desire they'd aroused in each other had flicked off as though he'd hit a circuit breaker. What was he thinking? she wondered. Conflicting messages flooded her, such as: how beautiful he was to her, even now, in his splendid isolation of mind, and how she could still taste the wonder of his mouth. And how much she wanted him back, touching, holding, loving her, all of it, she thought, her eyes flashing shut, *all of it.*

She found herself leaning against the door when the opposing arguments began to lay siege to her fantasies. Taking in his stormy profile, she realized he'd done it again. She was supposed to be ruthlessly investigating Nathanial Cutter—and what was she doing? Gazing at him as if he were Michelangelo's David. Once again, he'd waylaid her.

"How are you getting there?"

His question startled her. "To Belmont? I have a rental car. It's parked out front."

"It's going to rain," he said, leaning against the door-jamb. "The roads—they'll be bad."

He sounded so matter-of-fact, it was hard to tell if he was expressing polite concern or dabbling in sabotage. And it did look like rain. The skies were gunmetal gray. But then, around here the skies were almost always gunmetal gray. "I can handle it."

He swung around, and she could see by his expression that he'd made a decision. "I'm going with you. We'll take my car."

"Go with me? Why?"

"I know the way, the roads and the island."

Worried about her safety, was he? More likely he didn't want her on that island alone. Whatever his reasons, he didn't look like he could be talked out of them. A flat refusal on the tip of her tongue, she cocked her head and weighed her options. All things considered, it might be to her benefit to have him along.

Cutter's low-slung black Corvette ground gravel for twenty feet before he wheeled it out onto the two-lane highway to Belmont.

Chloe tightened her seat belt to keep from swaying toward her silent chauffeur. "I'm surprised you didn't have something better to do," she said, making conversation.

"As a matter of fact," he said, his eyes on the road ahead, "I had a date with one of the Dallas Cowboys' cheerleaders. I'm throwing her over to take you sightseeing."

"The team will be grateful." Chloe smiled, breathing a mental sigh of relief that his sense of humor was still intact.

Through the path the highway cut between spiraling evergreens, Chloe saw storm clouds roiling toward them. Black and full-bellied, they dominated the horizon, pierced by intermittent shafts of light that looked breathtakingly like pathways. To heaven or hell? she wondered nervously.

The building turbulence outside spiked the tension in the car as they roared down the highway. Acutely aware of their tight quarters, Chloe distracted herself with the problem of dealing with this unexpected turn of events.

She flinched at a sudden crack of thunder, and before she'd fully recovered, a solid sheet of rain encased them.

Cutter swore and slowed. "I'm turning back."

"No," she said with unusual force. She shook her head as he looked at her. "No—it'll blow over." A less determined woman would have agreed, but his tense behavior had confirmed her earlier hunch. This was no pleasure trip for him. He'd agreed to drive her for his own reasons, and she was sure she'd read the major reason accurately: he didn't want her on the island alone.

He's tripped himself up this time, she thought. If anyone on White Rock recognizes him, I'll know exactly who to question later.

She saw him gear down, felt the car slowing, swinging wide, and realized he was about to negotiate a U-turn. "No, Cutter," she cried, seizing his forearm. "I want to see that island. If you won't take me, I'll drive myself."

The moment of tension broke like a bowstring as he popped the gearshift into second, hit the gas pedal and swung the car back into the lane. "Why do you have to see island today?" he asked, his voice low as he accelerated into a wall of rain.

"I might not get another chance," she said, adding as he glanced at her, "I'll be going back soon, to New York." Hating the lies, but feeling an urgent need to stir his goodwill, she went on. "I'm a history buff." She recalled the tiny island museum the Chamber of Commerce rep had recommended, and she casually tossed out the name. "The place is loaded with artifacts and memorabilia—the sort of thing we history nuts can't resist."

He geared up suddenly, and she felt the movement of his muscles beneath her fingers. Startled at the sight of her hand still curled around his forearm, she withdrew it instantly, her fingers alive with the feel of him.

As they drove on, silenced by claps of thunder and wild rainfall, her sensitized nerves made her increasingly aware of the space that separated them—the half foot of charged air where his body left off and hers began.

She felt the restlessness in him; it was tangible. And other things, deeper, less physically evident, but even more implicit in his nature: loneliness, hunger and denial.

A guarded glance at him revealed emotions she hadn't expected. She saw vulnerability in the set of his jaw; she saw pride and a lonely kind of beauty. Her heart stirred with the desire to touch him.

Don't, she warned silently, knowing it wouldn't take much more than a touch to spark the tension between them.

Forcing her concentration back to the trip ahead, she caught the glint of eyes in her peripheral vision. Animal eyes, paralyzed, iced white by fear.

Cutter flinched and hit the brakes.

Slammed against the door by the force of the skidding car, Chloe heard the roar and whine of locked tires. She cringed, eyes squeezed shut, buffeted by the Corvette's tortured shimmying as it veered and spun in a half circle.

Nat's hands frantically worked the wheel. The car wrenched back, tires squealing, before he brought it to a grinding, sliding stop on the shoulder. He gripped the wheel reflexively, hard enough to snap it in half, and emitted a low curse.

The engine shuddered and died.

"What happened?" Chloe breathed.

"A deer." He exhaled again, audibly. "On the road. I hit the brakes too hard and the tires locked." He released the wheel and looked at her. After a moment he touched her shoulder, then ran his fingers along her cheek. "You okay?"

She nodded, and still he continued touching her as though to assure himself.

"We're going back," he stated flatly. But when he tried to start the car, the engine growled and died with each twist of the ignition key. Swearing softly, he got out and lifted the hood. After several moments, he was back, soaked to the skin. "It's the carburetor. You stay here. I'll go get help."

Watching his solitary stride as he headed back in the direction they'd come, Chloe felt a stab of guilt. He'd warned her about the weather. She hurriedly unfastened her seat belt, struggled out of the car and called his name. When he turned, she began to run.

"I'm coming with you," she said as she reached him. Drenched and gasping, she overrode his obviously pleased protests with an uncompromising shake of her head. "I got us into this," she said, walking beside him, "the least I can do is help get us out."

"God loves a persistent woman," he conceded finally, a smile touching his lips. His eyes held an iridescent sparkle. Enchanting, she thought as he took her hand.

He slowed his pace as they walked, urging her along with him at the same time. The deluge worsened, soaking them through to the skin, weighting their clothing, blinding them.

It seemed as though they'd walked all the way to the Maine-New Hampshire border when Chloe spotted a small sign telling them the Sunrise motel was half a mile down the road. They picked up the pace, and the last leg of their journey became a half-running, breathless rush for shelter.

The motel came into sight, its shingles bleached white by a simultaneous crack of thunder and lightning. The skies opened and roared. Instinctively, they began to sprint.

Spluttering water, panting like winded animals, they burst into her room and fell against the door. Chloe's lungs burned with each breath. Her heart throbbed in her ears. In the throes of recovery, she looked up at him as he looked down.

They acknowledged each other's condition breathlessly, water running through their hair, streaming down their faces. "It'll blow over?" Nat said, his voice cracking with disbelief. They began to laugh until, spurred by the sight of each other, they lost control. Chloe doubled, gurgling helplessly. Nat fell on the couch.

"I'll get some towels," she said finally, mustering some control, her voice still burbling with laughter as she headed for the bathroom. Barry Manilow was singing "Even Now" as she passed the dinette on her way and switched off the radio they'd forgotten all about.

She shed her sodden zip-up sweatshirt in the claw-footed bathtub, grabbed two large fluffy bathsheets and returned to the living room, still wearing a damp T-shirt and wet jeans.

She tossed him a towel and began vigorously to dry her own hair, still chuckling, only subliminally aware of his eyes on her. She had the chore nearly done before her subconscious snuck up on her. A spark of recognition ran along her spine. He wasn't moving; he was watching her. Not moving... watching.

Her hands stilled, poised above her head, her fingers entangled in the towel. She raised her eyes, saw where his gaze was fixed, and felt a hot flush of surprise.

Following his eyes, she looked down. Her damp T-shirt clung wantonly to the fullness of her breasts, revealing creamy flesh in patches, catching every movement. She lowered her arms with exaggerated care, dropped the towel and finally, her heart fluttering in her throat, she raised her eyes to his.

His features were taut, expectant, his eyes as black as passion itself.

"I'd better get these wet clothes off," she said, aware of the throaty swell in her voice.

He nodded, hesitating where he stood.

As she started for the bathroom, he called her name with such low force that she shuddered to a stop.

"Stay here," he said, the undercurrent in his words holding her like a physical restraint. She felt a crazy siphoning off of energy, felt the muscles in her legs quiver like water.

His voice vibrated through her. "Stay here, Chloe... where I can see you."

"Cutter," she rasped, her voice tightening as she realized what he wanted. "I can't."

She stared at the door to the bathroom and knew she had to get there somehow, but she couldn't move. With a sharp intake of air she tried to block out what was happening inside her—the climbing excitement, the breathless whispers.

She felt his eyes on her back, saw them in her mind. Dark and haunting, they drew her irresistibly. Convulsing with an exquisite shiver, she felt it begin... *surrender*.

"Chloe."

"I can't," she heard herself say, and yet she came around, still shaking her head, her arms spontaneously crossing in front of her, her fingers grasping the bottom of her T-shirt. I can't, she thought, her body racked with sweet pain. A cry caught in her throat as she gathered the material up with trembling fingers and lifted....

Nat Cutter watched her tug her T-shirt up and felt a spasm lock his throat. The soft freefall of her breasts as the damp material cleared sent a knifelike pain through him.

She pulled the shirt free of her head and let it drop. Her breath caught; it sounded like a soft sob.

"My God," he whispered, watching her.

Her skin was a shade paler than English cream, her breasts were swollen. Even the fanning delicacy of her lifting eyelashes entranced him. They were dark and as lush as a rain forest. She looked up at him, and his heart bucked.

He reached her in two strides, groaning as he touched her. "You're beautiful," he said, his voice husky, "so beautiful."

The faintest quiver of a smile touched her lips.

He gathered her in his arms, acutely aware of the pressure of her breasts against his rib cage. A sound broke inside him, low, serrated with need. Working his fingers deep into the wild red halo of curls, he breathed kisses over her eyes, cheeks, lips.

He drew his hand around to cup a breast, and its heat sparked nerve endings that ran clear up his arm. "You feel like a dream," he said, soft and harsh against her lips.

His other hand found the waistband of her jeans. Hearing her soft gasp, he began to whisper to her, soothingly, low and seductive, ignoring the rigidity building in her body.

"Wait," she pleaded as he freed the snap.

Caught up in a mindless rush, he began to lower the zipper.

"*Wait,*" she said, pulling back.

He scanned her face. She was rigid, trembling like a leaf beneath his hands. "What is it?"

Her head jerked in mute denial.

She was frightened, he could see that in the way she held herself. Not the kind of fear a woman might feel with a new man, this was something stronger. Mixed with it he saw other emotions: confusion, embarrassment, anger...even some shame?

The realization, when it came to him, was sudden and incredulous. A blow to his gut. *"This is your first time, isn't it?"*

"No," she said, looking away. "Of course not."

He caught her chin and drew her back. "Listen to me, Chloe, I need to know." Ease up, Cutter, he told himself. "You've never been with a man before, have you?" he asked more gently.

Her eyes were huge. Their soft desperation cut into him. She dropped her head finally, shook it slowly. "Almost," she said, as though to herself, "in college."

"Almost?" He groaned, shutting his eyes. *Almost didn't count.* "Why didn't you tell me?"

She broke from him and half turned away. "I didn't think it would matter."

"Didn't think—My God, Chloe, it *does*."

He barely heard her whispered "Why?"

"Because—" He riffled his hands through his hair, swung around, walking to the window. "Because I can't be the one to—" He'd never felt such agonizing confusion. The words weren't there. "The first time has to be right," he told her, his voice taut, "the right man."

"And if I want it to be with you?"

Desire beat inside him, but he couldn't. *He couldn't.*

Fighting to control the ache in his gut the only way he knew how, he walked to her and brought her face up, his hands framing her throat in a roughened caress. "You don't know me. You don't know what I am." His heart hardened against the soft pull of her eyes. "I'm the kind of man your mother warned you against."

Feeling the quiver of her jaw beneath his fingers, he added heartlessly, "You're no match for me, Chloe. You and I are like a predator and its prey."

She tried to pull away, but he jerked her back. "Have you ever seen a cat with a moth? The cat watches, fascinated with the moth's quivering movement . . . and then it strikes. It has to," he grated softly. "Predators are fated to destroy soft, vulnerable things."

He saw the dull shock of fear in her eyes and knew that he'd won. Or had he lost? His heart a stone in his chest, he swung around and strode toward the door.

Six

Chloe skipped a stone across the nearly placid water. Above her a magnificent barrier of cloud cover, fluffy and shock-white, blocked off the deepening indigo of the early-evening sky. Oddly, the serenity intensified her restlessness.

The harsh jangling of a telephone climbed her spine.

Him? Heart quickening, she turned and started back to her room. The way he'd stormed out that morning, she'd never expected to hear from him again.

Giving her door a quick nudge shut as she passed it, she picked up the receiver, held it in both hands for a minute, then brought it to her ear. "Hello," she said, aware of her own breath against the mouthpiece.

"Ms. Kates?" a masculine voice asked.

Confusion and disappointment flooded her. "Yes?"

"Gordon Browne calling, your stepfather's assistant."

"Oh... yes." She'd detected something familiar in the stilted style. "What is it, Mr. Browne?" In the years since she'd left Northpointe, she and the formidable Gordon Browne had never even come close to a first-name basis relationship. Not that she'd wanted one—his vigilant features had always put her off—but still, it was curious. "Is everything all right?" she asked, suddenly concerned that her stepfather's condition had worsened.

"Fine, Ms. Kates. Mr. Guthrie's made some progress since your visit to the hospital. He might be able to return home soon."

"Oh, that's good," she said, relieved.

"Not to Northpointe, of course. He's taken a suite at a hotel near the hospital. Actually, it's something else I've called you about. I was wondering if anything had changed since we talked. Regarding Sara, that is."

A fundamental question pushed through Chloe's surprise. How had Browne tracked her down? The only person she'd told about Maine was Marsha, and even her partner didn't know the real reason for the trip.

"Sara?" she murmured, stalling. She wasn't sure why she still felt the need to keep a lid on her investigation of Cutter. It was a hunch, but such a strong one she went with it. "Why do you ask, Mr. Browne? And I'm curious. How did you find me?"

For the first time ever, she thought she heard him falter. "I—well, I called your office, of course. Your partner was good enough to tell me how to reach you."

"I see." The awkward silence that followed stirred an idea. "I'd like very much to help find Sara. Perhaps if you told me what you know about her disappearance." The subtle challenge had been on her mind ever since the hospital visit when she began to suspect Guthrie and Browne of holding something back. She'd always assumed it was Guthrie's paranoia about the press that led him to hush up the incident at Northpointe. But maybe...

"Ms. Kates," Browned chastised, ignoring her questions, "Mr. Guthrie's health and advanced years made it imperative that we locate his daughter without delay. He was hoping you might have been in touch with her."

The flicker of passion in his voice increased Chloe's wariness. "I haven't, really. I would have told you." At least the first part of the answer was true.

"You're sure? If there's anything you know, anything you could do—"

"I'd do it," she assured him quickly.

"We thought your trip—" he pressed stiffly. "Well, Maine this time of year is hardly a vacation spot. We thought you had some other reason for going."

Cat and mouse, she thought, frustrated. We're both playing it. Why? And why didn't she trust him? A ripple crossed her shoulder blades as it occurred to her that he and Guthrie might be using her somehow, might even be shadowing her. Lord, that was farfetched. Now *she* was getting paranoid. "It's quiet here," she said, "and I needed some R and R."

"You're vacationing alone, Ms. Kates?"

"Yes," she said instantly—and then wished she'd told him to mind his own business. "I'll be in touch, Mr. Browne," she informed him briskly, "if I should have anything to tell you." Cutting off his attempt to detain her with a polite goodbye, she hung up the phone.

A half hour later, she'd nearly worn a path in the linoleum, pacing, wondering if she'd done the right thing. Fourteen years ago she'd held back the truth about Joshua, now she was doing the same thing with Cutter. And all because of some nagging intuition?

Reasons pushed through her rising disquiet. She was protecting Cutter because he was her only link to Sara...and because if she admitted her suspicions to Browne, he would almost certainly sic detectives on Cutter. And that would make Cutter murderous. And what if he wasn't Joshua? Or if he *had* done something wrong . . . ?

Anxiety high in her chest, she closed her eyes and saw Nat Cutter's features there, indistinct at first, coming into focus like a photograph developing. With sudden and stunning clarity, she saw the taut, expectant lines, the blinding flash of passion in his eyes. "Sweet heaven," she breathed, crossing her arms to subside her heart's burst of speed.

Eyes blinking open, she glimpsed herself in the vanity across the room and walked slowly toward the image. Is that me? she questioned, astonished by the strained and tousled figure she saw reflected in the mirror. Her clothes awry, her hair as wild as Cutter's hands had left it, she felt as though she were staring at someone else, a woman out of control. *Is that me?*

Huge green eyes stared back at her, full of conflicting needs and confusion. That woman in the mirror looked caught—on the verge of something crazy.

Releasing a breath, Chloe turned away. "It's time to get honest," she told herself unsteadily, putting some distance between herself and the vanity. "You're not handling this well. You're not handling it at *all*. You came here to find Sara, but this thing with Cutter, this *obsession*—" she purposely emphasized the word to shock some sense into that woman in the mirror "—it's taking over."

She went on, merciless now. "You've fouled up plan after plan, bungled almost every opportunity. You haven't got the vaguest idea what to do next—" A knot drew tight in her stomach as she realized how true it was. Cutter had some kind of hold on her, almost hypnotic, a power she couldn't fight. He blunted her natural instincts, continually had her at cross-purposes with herself, and worst of all—her eyes returned irresistibly to the mirror—he aroused her.

The morning's encounter played through her mind in shocking detail: the whispering impulses that had compelled her to undress, the thrill of his hands on her body, the breathless touch of his lips. If he hadn't backed off what would she have done?

You couldn't have stopped him, the mirror image warned. He's in your blood, has taken possession of your senses. You would have done anything, *anything he wanted*.

"I'm in over my head," she whispered, a tremor in her voice. As the realization that she was truly out of control registered in every nerve ending, a drastic solution came to her. "Browne...call Browne back...*tell him the truth.*"

The green eyes flashed no, unequivocally, *no*.

"Why not?" Chloe whispered, turning away. Gordon Browne was a competent man; he'd been loyal to Guthrie. He'd never actually done anything to confirm her suspicions. The distrust she felt might be nothing more than her imagination working overtime again. She had Sara to think of—and Guthrie. How could she justify holding back what she knew under the circumstances?

The more she considered the idea, the less desperate it seemed. She turned away, her eyes fixing on the phone. I'll tell him to be discreet, hire the best, she thought. Cutter mustn't know he's being investigated. Exhaling, she walked toward the table. And if Browne learns something, *anything*, he's to report to me first, before he takes any action. "If he doesn't agree to those terms," she resolved aloud, "I won't do it."

Her fingers touched the receiver, and a shock ran up her arm. She froze in place as a vivid snapshot from the past rushed at her: a frightened twelve-year-old confronted by the police, Guthrie foaming with rage, savage dogs that tore people apart. *Joshua. Was she turning the dogs loose on him?*

She forced the images from her mind and stared at the phone, startled at how sinister its bulky, old-fashioned lines suddenly seemed.

"All right," she said finally, exhaling as she turned to face her mirror image. "All right—you win. One more day. Twenty-four hours. But that's all. If I haven't turned anything up by then, I'm going to call Gordon Browne."

Muffled voices touched Chloe's sleep-hazed mind, registering somewhere in her subconscious. She opened her eyes with some effort, gradually aware that she'd drifted off. Blinking to bring the wall clock into focus, she realized it was nearly midnight. The moment she'd taken to rest and recharge had stretch to two or three hours.

Barefoot, but still fully dressed, she pushed herself up, groaning as she slid off the bed. Her eyes burned; her throat felt scratchy. Chalking it up to that morning's run in the rain, she focused in on the radio's soft blare. That's what she'd heard, she realized, starting for it.

As her fingers touched the switch, a distant clicking sound caught her ear. *The sound of a door opening.* Her senses sharpened, cutting through the last residues of sleep. The noise came from her left—Cutter's room. She opened her own door and edged out, squinting to see in the damp, nearly opaque air.

A quiver of movement, a scuffling sound drew her focus.

Her eyes strained for definition, and abruptly, as they adjusted to the darkness, she saw him. A silhouette, black on black, pulled Cutter's door shut noiselessly. Instinctively, Chloe slipped back into the shadowed recesses of her own doorway where he couldn't see her.

Cutter? she questioned as the man darted past, his head angled away, his jet hair flying. Suppressing an impulse to call out the name, she watched him stride up the pathway that edged the bluffs.

She watched him until the darkness swallowed him, shook off her uncertainty and bolted in pursuit.

Frigid onshore gusts blew her hair and burned her cheeks as she reached the bluffs and continued on, her breath coming faster. Tiny pebbles cut into her bare soles, and a sickle moon, shrouded by mists, provided so little light that she blundered off the path constantly.

He came into her sights around the next turn, and she slowed immediately. The path's ultimate destination was Johnson's Cove, a quiet little harbor she'd seen pictures of on the wall of the office the day she registered. Why would he be heading there?

He picked up his pace, and she broke into a trot, increasing her speed steadily to keep up. Suddenly he was running as though he'd heard her. She sprinted in pursuit, her pulse rate soaring as she veered to avoid a murky obstacle.

He glanced back, and she feinted aside, snagging something with her foot. Suddenly she was off balance, reeling forward. Her hands and knees hit the ground first, jarring her whole body with shock.

"Damn," she gasped, staggering, fighting dizziness as she pushed herself up. Watching him disappear around a curve ahead, she fought to quiet the roaring in her head and regain her equilibrium.

In the hair's-breadth silence between shock and action, a sound pricked her ears. The sickening crackle of leaves underfoot. It came from behind. Her heart rocketing, she heard it again and turned, gasping as shadows dropped down, as dark and shivery as living things.

The wind, the trees, she realized.

Five feet in front of her she saw a jagged cavity in the rocks and froze in a panicky examination of its black depths. A claustrophobic feeling engulfed her, the premonition of something unseen, drawing near. Tiny prickles raised the hair on her nape. He'd seen her, whoever he was. Had he doubled back?

An energy, like phosphorescence, irradiated the chasm's darkness. Chloe's stomach spasmed with fear. "Who's there?"

The movement of something human, *the glint of eyes, milk white in the darkness*, shocked her senses. A memory pierced the night. She'd seen those eyes before—when she'd been a child, lost in the woods, terrified by the image of a hovering demon. The old terror moved through her, paralyzing her legs as she tried to back away. "Who's there?"

As he stepped out of the shadows, the moon flared to a silver brightness, its light running in his hair.

"Joshua?"

Lightheadedness swept her senses.

She saw him coming toward her through a veil of time-blurred space. Dancing phantoms, shot through with oblique light, revealed haunting glimpses of his features. At the last minute, she looked away.

A hand bracketed her jaw, brought her face up. "What did you call me?" His harsh inquiry broke the spell.

"Cutter?" she whispered, staring up at him. Not Joshua, Nat Cutter, of course, *of course*. What in God's name was happening to her? "But you—?" She broke off, looking up the path, seeing only empty space. Her head snapped back. "What are you doing here?"

He took hold of her shoulders as though he meant to shake some sense into her. "Me? What are *you* doing here? Half frozen, shivering." He looked down. "And barefoot?"

"I heard something, someone. I just wanted to—"

His narrowing eyes silenced her. "What did you call me?"

"Call you?" Had she said the name out loud? "I don't ... remember," she hedged. "I was frightened."

He studied her face for a moment, or it could have been several; she lost track of time in the wake of his searching inquiry. If he saw the lie, he didn't acknowledge it. Touching a finger to her cheek, he thrilled her gently with a caress. A spark that could have been pain, or passion, glinted in his eyes.

She felt the jerk of his hand as he pulled away, saw his features tighten into a grimace. "Do you have any idea what you're getting into?" he said, the question laced with threat.

"What do you mean?"

He shook his head. "You really don't know, do you?"

"I know I won't be frightened off by your threats," she said, her spine stiffening at the "hopeless child" tone in his voice. "And I also know I can take care of myself."

"No, dammit, you can't." His hand came up, raked through his hair in a gesture that twitched with controlled violence. "You're headed for more trouble than you could ever imagine."

She met his eyes and defied him. "Meaning yourself?"

"Meaning *trouble* in the larger sense—meaning those who play with fire get burned. You're playing with fire, Chloe. You're going to get hurt, and I don't mean a broken heart."

They stared at each other, eyes flashing. Deadlocked.

"I don't know why you're here," he said finally. "But if it's because of me, then please—give it up. I'm not what you need, I never will be—"

"*Stop* telling me what I need," she cut back, her voice low. "And stop presuming that it's *you*."

As she pulled free of his grasp and shouldered away, he caught her wrist and whipped her around. "I'm doing you a favor, dammit. I'm telling you to get out of here. Go home."

"Save the favors."

Steel fingers stung her wrist and then released. "What's with you? A self-destructive streak? A death wish?"

A hot spark of anger and a crazy need to best him, *just once*, spurred her on. "You want me to leave Maine, Cutter? Give me a reason. Come on," she challenged, swiping at him, crooking a finger, "a real reason. Tell me why I should go, and none of this broken heart business, because I'm not the soft touch you think I am. I can play hardball, Cutter. Try me."

"I don't know what you're talking about," he said, so low she could barely hear him. "But I'm not talking any more, I'm telling you. Catch a flight to New York tomorrow. If you don't, I'll—"

"What?" she said, fighting the tremor of fear that assaulted her. "You'll what?"

His eyes deflected moonlight like a cat's. "Be on that plane," was all he said. Wheeling around, he started up the path to Johnson's Cove.

"Where are you going?" she called after him.

"You said you saw somebody. I'm going to check it out." Halting midstride, he jerked around, each word a whip crack. "Get out of here, Chloe. Go home."

It wasn't him she'd been following? Watching him disappear, she felt a delayed reaction of trembling wash her body like the hot chill of a fever. *Go home?* Not on your sweet life, mister, she thought, shivering violently. Instinct told her she was close to what she'd come for, *very close*.

Heat burned Chloe's cheeks and stung at her closed eyelids. She turned restively, opened her eyes and saw pale morning sunshine filtering through the dust-streaked window.

Awareness came gradually. She'd made a valiant effort to stay awake last night, intending to be up when Cutter returned, but racking chills and exhaustion had drugged her into a restless sleep. Pressing a palm to her forehead, she felt the shock of cool skin against hot.

The telephone clanged impatiently.

Cutter, she supposed, not at all sure she had the strength to face him.

"I'm coming," she grumbled, as the merciless clanging continued. Swaying dizzily, she made it to the table and picked up the phone.

"Get on a plane, Chloe," her partner, Marsha, was yelling. "Come back to New York. Come back immediately!"

"Marsha? What's wrong?"

"Nothing's wrong, everything's *right*. This proves it, Chloe. This proves there is a God."

Chloe sat down heavily, her legs unsteady. "Slow down. What's happened?"

"You know how long we've been struggling to make it as publicists? To get this agency out of the red?"

"Yes..."

"And how I've tried to talk you into asking your stepfather for a loan, but you wouldn't do it because you've always felt like a charity case? And how determined you are to prove you can make it on your own?"

"Marsha," she coaxed weakly, knowing how her partner loved a big buildup, "please—get to the point."

"And how we've been waiting for the phone to ring, for that big break?"

"*Marsha.*"

"Our big break just called."

"Who? Who called?" Ignoring her shaky legs, Chloe grabbed up the telephone and walked until the short cord jerked her back.

"Syd Reinhardt. You know—the agent—the one who's organizing the writers' conference this weekend. Sit down, Chloe, you're not going to believe this. They want a speaker from our agency."

Astonished, Chloe returned to the chair and collapsed. Yes, she knew Syd Reinhardt. His agency was fast becoming one of the largest and most prestigious in New York. His authors were big names, bestsellers, but like all shrewd agents, Syd had a warmup bullpen of brilliant rookies, future stars who needed plenty of publicity to build name recognition. What a source of referrals! The Reinhardt logo was *gold*. Just to be able to say they were associated with that agency could put them on the map!

"Chloe? You there?"

She hugged the phone to her stomach. "Marsha, are you sure?"

"Absolutely. One of Syd's people called today. Said he was sorry about the last-minute notice, but somebody got sick and left a hole in their conference schedule."

A delighted smile and sigh of relief welled at the same time. "You're going to be terrific, Marsha. I wish I could be there to hear you."

"Me? Chloe, they want *you*!"

"What? Why?"

"Darned if I know, but they want you and only you. Syd's personal request."

"Personal request?" Chloe's heart began to thump. What did that mean? She tried to stand up and couldn't.

"Sorry about your R and R," Marsha was saying, "but you've got to get the first plane back. You're the opening speaker."

First plane back? Opening speaker? No, not now. She couldn't leave *now*. The chair scraped across the floor as she finally made it to her feet. "I can't, Marsha."

"Can't? What do you mean can't?"

"I can't do it. I can't come home right now, there's a problem here. Listen, you cover for me. You're a better speaker than I am, anyway."

She heard an uncharacteristic gasp at the other end of the line. "What's got into you? I told you—they don't want me, they want *you*." Building up steam, her partner added in typical Marsha, lay-'em-out-flat style, "If you care anything about me, about this agency, about staying *alive*, you'll get back here, Chloe. Pronto!"

Holding the phone away, her hand over the mouthpiece, Chloe tried to clear her fevered brain and consider her options. It only took her a moment to come to grips with the fact that she had to go. The agency meant everything to her. Not only was it her shot at independence and security, but she and Marsha had put heart and soul into building it into a viable business.

Yes, she had to go, but dammit, *she couldn't leave*. Lord, she groaned, a rock and a hard place would be heaven compared to this.

Ignoring Marsha's repeated "Chloe!" which filtered through her fingers, she finally hit on the only possible solution. "Okay, I'll be there, Marsha," she promised. "I'll catch the first flight back."

Pressing the disconnect button over her partner's moans of relief, she began to dial the airlines. Feverish chills forced her to concentrate. Cutter would think he'd scared her off, and maybe that was just as well. He'd never expect her to catch a plane back to Maine tomorrow, and if she was careful, he'd never know she'd returned.

She still had twelve hours left of the twenty-four hours she'd promised herself. Without Cutter running interference, that should be more than enough time for a thorough casing of White Rock Island.

Seven

Chloe stood offstage, hovering in the wings, while Syd Reinhardt welcomed the packed auditorium to the Tenth Annual Atlantic States Writers' Conference. "A record crowd," she heard the prematurely graying superagent tell his audience.

Listening to him introduce some of the more sterling members of the literary community—publishers, editors and writers of note—Chloe closed her eyes and prayed for strength. In a few minutes he'd be introducing her. Chloe Kates, virtually unknown publicist, untested public speaker, owner of watery knees and a fevered brow. Her throat felt like rusty steel wool. Even two industrial strength aspirin hadn't dulled the five-foot-three-inch toothache her body had become. Why hadn't Syd asked Marsha? Marsha loved to talk. Marsha never stopped talking!

Last night was a good example, Chloe thought ironically. From the moment her partner had picked her up at the airport, Marsha'd barely stopped for a breath until they reached the two bedroom sublet flat they shared in the Grammercy Park area. Besides giving Chloe a running commentary on the events of the past few days, she'd repeatedly pointed out what Chloe already knew—that Reinhardt's conference was their "ticket to ride."

"Wipe that glazed expression from your face," she'd urged desperately. "You've got to impress Syd Reinhardt even if that means cartwheeling onto the stage. Energy, Chloe, *energy*."

Chloe hadn't found the right moment to tell her partner that the speech she'd prepared on the plane was certain to "impress" Syd, whether favorably or not was the question!

"Our first speaker," Syd was saying, "represents an innovative new agency here in New York. Not content with being 'just a publicist,' this woman is a creative strategist, a risk taker, and a businesswoman on the cutting edge of change. With a finger on current trends and a focus on the future, she and her partner are turning their agency into a high-velocity publicity machine...."

Chloe listened, stunned. Having only met Syd Reinhardt in the most casual sense at mutual business functions, she couldn't imagine where he'd come up with those superlatives... unless he'd been talking to Marsha, too. She took a deep breath and held her hand to her forehead. *What doesn't kill me makes me stronger.*

"How about a big welcome for Chloe Katherine Kates!" He even knew her middle name?

The audience thundered out applause. Adrenaline spurred Chloe into action. She walked onto the stage, rubbery-legged, an overlarge smile on her face.

"Thank you," she gushed nervously. "Any chance you're looking for work?" she quipped as she took the mike from Syd. "After that intro, I'd like to sign you up."

The audience tittered and went silent as she turned to face them, a thousand eyes trained on her. "What does it take to be a best-selling author in the eighties?" she asked, wishing she didn't sound so short of breath. "Talent? Persistence? Luck?"

Seeing heads begin to nod, she raised a hand. "If your answer is none of the above, you're right." She looked around the room and saw what she expected—surprise, skepticism. "Talent and persistence still count for a lot, of course, but this is the media decade, the television generation is coming of age and today's formula *and* shortcut to success is 'hype.' Not a pretty word, but if you're in a hurry—and who isn't in the eighties—it works and it's fast."

Stopping to clear her throat, she realized her hushed voice had them straining to hear. "With the right book—and by 'right' I don't mean good, there are plenty of bad bestsellers out there—I'm talking about a workable concept, an idea that captures the public's imagination. With that kind of a concept and a full-tilt ad campaign, you can guarantee yourself a bestseller."

She had them. Some eyes were wider, some narrower, but she had them. Now, all she had to do was back up her extravagant claim. Her voice getting huskier by the minute, she explained how a clever publicity campaign could put any book on the bestseller list, even a distinctly bad one. "You've all read them," she said, "the books that are so marginal you wonder why one copy sold, much less the one hundred thousand or so it took to put them on a bestseller list. Why do you buy them? The same reason everyone else does. Because you saw a flashy television spot or a full-page print ad. You were drawn in by a big money ad campaign."

Aches and pains forgotten, she went on, talking with more energy and animation as she explained how the right combination of packaging and promotion could make even a dull read sound dazzling. Seeing the heads begin to nod as she backed up her claims with cost-comparison data and industry statistics, she realized how good it felt to be back on her own turf, *sane again*, and effective.

She went on to warn them that even though "bestsellerdom" could be bought once, or maybe even twice, a series of terrible books could ruin even the most highly-financed career.

"The most important bit of advice I can give you today," she told them sincerely, "is to put heart and soul into your work. *Don't shortchange your readers.* Write the best book you know how, and then promote it. If you can't afford to hire a professional, do it on your own, and don't be bashful. If you love the story, that's reason enough to promote it."

High on a wave of audience approval, she went on to outline a step-by-step course of self-promotion and finally summed up her talk with a brief rundown of the services her agency provided.

The applause was loud, long and deeply gratifying.

Breathing out a sigh of relief, Chloe asked for questions. As hands went up, she saw Syd Reinhardt at the back of the hall standing near the entrance.

Her heart nearly stopped. Was the man next to him a trick of her overstimulated brain? Nat Cutter glanced up from his conversation with Syd, and his dark gaze brushed over her—lightly, but with enough force to make her feel like she'd been zapped by a live wire.

Shock brought a wave of feverish light-headedness. She grabbed for the podium and held on, aware that hands were waving at her. What was he doing here?

"Yes," she rasped, responding to a man in the front row who called out, "Ms. Kates?" to get her attention. She tried to muster the presence of mind to answer his question, but the words kept trailing off. Even in a packed auditorium, Nat Cutter drew her like a negative charge attracts a positive one.

She wrenched her eyes away from Cutter and nodded at a woman waving several rows back. "Next question."

"You look so young," the woman remarked. "How long have you been a publicist, and how did you get your start?"

"Three years—or has it been—uh, no, yeah, three years." Aware that she was stumbling, Chloe compensated with an energetic smile. "My journalism professor convinced me I had a flair for public relations and volunteered me for the staff of the university yearbook. The rest," she said, her attention darting back to Cutter, "is history."

Leaning against the back wall, no longer talking to Syd, Cutter looked like a figure out of time—as though he might always have been there, all his life, all eternity, just waiting for her to look his way. Their gaze touched, and for an instant everything stopped.

He acknowledged her, not with a smile or a nod, but with his eyes. An energy connected them, penetrating her so deeply she felt it like a physical tug.

"Ms. *Kates,*" someone called out. Chloe jerked in the direction of the voice and saw a heavyset man coming to his feet. "Has your agency ever promoted a book that made the bestseller list?"

With Cutter hovering in the background, Chloe described promotional campaigns for a pop psychology text and a science-fiction series. "And we're currently working on several—" she stopped midsentence to watch as Cutter straightened and began to walk toward the door "—other projects," she said faintly. *Don't leave.*

His hand hit the door and she heard herself whispering "Wait." The impulse to break away and follow him moved through her like physical pain. Explaining that her time was up, she began to back away from the podium, thanking the audience several times through a last wave of applause.

A short flight of steps backstage took her down to the auditorium. She hurried up the aisle, acknowledged a scattering of compliments, and pushed through the auditorium doors. It only took moments to confirm her fear that he'd left. Finding no sign of him anywhere in the marble halls, she returned, spotted Syd Reinhardt in the midst of a cluster of conferees and headed for him.

"Could I speak to you a minute?" she asked, standing on her tiptoes and signaling to him.

"Sure," he called back, working his way through the crowds. "Great speech," he said as he reached her.

"Thanks." Smiling, she urged him away from the confusion. "And thank you for making it possible," she added when they found a quiet spot. "While I was talking I saw a man standing next to you. I wanted to speak with him but it looks like he's already left."

"You mean Nat Cutter?"

"Yes, do you know him?"

"Know him?" Syd grimaced in mock despair. "Cutter's responsible for most of my misspent youth. We went to Harvard together, Nat and I, both bent on becoming the great American novelist. He did it, and I did the next best thing. I represent him."

"Really?" was all she could say.

Reinhardt's steel blue eyes regarded her. "You a friend, too?"

"Yes," she said hesitantly. Misspent youth? She was staring at a storehouse of information! "Actually, I'm Harvard, too—" As soon as she said it, she realized Marsha had probably provided him with a bio that declared her an NYU alumnus.

"That right?" Syd smiled. "One of the walking wounded?"

"Just flesh wounds," she clarified quickly. "I only took a graduate class or two."

They both laughed, and Reinhardt folded his arms, adding, "Yeah, Nat's quite a character. We go way back, fraternity brothers."

Chloe nodded subtle encouragement. "Then you probably remember Evans Cole?"

"Oh God, yeah," he chuckled. "Cole nearly flunked me out of his class. Great days those were. Nat and I and two other guys from the frat took off right after graduation, toured Europe, rode the trains, slept in flophouses."

"I always wanted to do that," she said sincerely. "Were you there long?"

"Me?" He shook his head. "Three months. Nat stayed on though. He met his wife there, of course."

Chloe nearly staggered. "Wife?"

"Yeah, Elena." He looked at her oddly. "Hasn't he ever told you about her? But you must know the story of Nat and Elena. It was in all the papers."

"I—yes, of course."

"God, what a tragedy that was." Sadness briefly touched Syd's features. "She was so young."

Fighting to hold herself steady, Chloe tried to assimilate what she'd just heard. Nat had been married? Her brain refused to accept the information.

"They'd only been together three or four years. Police never did figure out whether it was an accident or a suicide."

Chloe's head snapped up. "She's dead?"

"Yeah, of course. Ten years ago." He considered her, questions in his eyes. "How long have you known Nat?"

"Elena Fiori?" she whispered, remembering suddenly.

As Syd nodded, the newspaper accounts of the drowning of the young Italian film ingenue who'd been married to an American writer began to surface in Chloe's mind. "Yes, of course, Elena." Despite her shock, some lowest common denominator of logic kept her talking. "I guess he—Nat—doesn't like to talk about her, or that time."

"No, he doesn't, you're right," Syd agreed. "I think the scars are still there. He held himself responsible."

"But he *wasn't*, of course."

"No," Syd affirmed. "Only in that he never should have married her in the first place. Elena had deep problems, but Nat wouldn't be talked out of her. He was into rescuing people in those days, and she was a beautiful girl, lonely despite all her fame. She had that wounded animal quality so irresistible to a man like him."

Half listening, Chloe managed to ask over the dull thud of her heart, "You said you and Nat left for Europe right after graduation?"

At his nod, Chloe felt a slow, cold realization taking hold, a kind of psychic numbing as her mind registered each successive bit of information. Nat Cutter was in Europe when Sara disappeared. In Europe and either married, or about to be married to another woman. He couldn't have been at Northpointe. And then came the final jolt to her nervous system. *He wasn't the man she'd seen.*

She stepped back, and Syd reached out to steady her. "Are you all right?"

Through a rush of heat and lassitude, she shook her head. "No, no, I don't think so. I've been sick the past few days, and all this excitement—I think I'd better go."

"Sure, I'll come with you, get you a cab," he said, taking hold of her arm and walking her out of the auditorium. "You sure you're going to be okay?"

She nodded, and when they reached the street, she thanked him again for everything.

"I should be thanking you," he told her, "for getting the conference off to a good start." He hailed a cab and turned back to her as it sped on by. "And by the way, your agency intrigues me. I've taken on a couple of new writers who'll need some PR. You interested?"

"Yes," she said, without a second's hesitation.

"Good. I'll be in touch, then. Actually, my Manhattan office uses Dillon and Paine, but I'm in the process of opening up a second office near Grammercy Park, not too far from you. We'll be signing up new talent every week." He shrugged, smiled pleasantly. "Who knows, maybe we can work something out."

At last her heart began to beat normally again. "I hope so," she said, thanking him with a valiant smile.

A taxi roared up to the curb. Opening the door, he helped her inside. "Take care of that fever," he said, shutting the door and waving.

She waved back, wondering briefly as the taxi pulled away how he'd known she had a fever.

The excitement of Syd Reinhardt's offer evaporated like steam in the first few minutes of the trip back to the office Chloe shared with her partner. Alone, and feeling oddly isolated in the back seat of the cab, she worked to make sense of what she'd learned. "I believed he was Joshua," she said, wondering how her own instincts could have betrayed her so totally, "I really did." She felt as though she'd been told her green eyes were brown, looked in a mirror and discovered it true.

Disbelief welled up. "I couldn't have been that wrong," she mumbled, numbed by indisputable facts. Nat Cutter was in Europe when Sara disappeared . . . in Europe and in love with another woman.

"We're here, lady," the cabbie informed her.

She found a bill in her purse, handed it to him unsteadily and got out of the cab.

"Lady? Your change?" he called after her.

"Keep it," she said, not quite sure how much she'd given him. Moving more out of habit than conscious intention, she walked to the elevator and pressed the fourth-floor button.

Marsha was there, talking on the phone and pacing as Chloe entered their tiny two-room suite of offices. "I've got him booked on Merv Griffin and I'm working on Donahue," she said, talking into the receiver tucked under her chin as she leafed through a file.

The familiar chaos jarred Chloe momentarily. This was the real world, her office, where she belonged. Yet, looking around the room, she took in the cluttered desk and stuffed file cabinets with a sense of alienation, as though something fundamental had changed. She felt as if she'd come out of a dark dream...and into a waking world that wasn't the way she'd left it.

It's me, this damnable fever, she thought, a dizzying throb setting in just above her eyes.

Forcing herself to wave and wink as Marsha looked up, she continued on through the front office, entered her own work area and set her briefcase on the floor. Everything looked exactly as she'd left it, with the exception of several haphazardly stacked piles of mail on her desk.

She began to sort through the first stack, her fingers working, her mind held by a question lurking in its shadows. Was she going back to Maine?

"Tell me everything!" a voice squealed from behind. Her partner rushed into the room. "How'd you do? What happened?"

"Did great," Chloe said, looking up with a nod and a tight-lipped smile.

"Great?" Marsha breathed, bubbling with excitement. "What does that mean in round figures?"

"Two referrals now, more to come if we hustle. Reinhardt's opening a new office. He implied he might use our agency exclusively."

"Oh my Gawd!" Marsha twirled and dropped into the chair opposite Chloe's desk. "I'm overcome."

Chloe felt a grin flicker. Thank God for Marsha, she thought, her mood easing a little. Her partner's enthusiasm was as infectious as ever. "I was hoping for speechless," she said dryly.

"What did you *do*?" Marsha's tone implied Chloe might have bargained with the devil or something equally unspeakable to make this deal.

"Darned if I know," Chloe said truthfully. "Maybe I was in the right place at the right time."

The telephone shrilled on the desk behind Chloe. Startled, she jerked around and stared at it, her face draining of color.

Marsha jumped up to answer it. "Order's ready? Thanks," she said and hung up. "That was the printer about our new brochures." She stared at Chloe curiously. "What's wrong with you?"

The throb above Chloe's eyes flared, pulsating in her temples. "It startled me, that's all. I'm not feeling well—"

Marsha took hold of Chloe's shoulders and inspected her like a concerned mother. "Look at me," she insisted. When Chloe did, Marsha clucked softly. "Uh-oh—I see unrequited love in those eyes.... It's a man, isn't it?"

"Marsha, let go of me."

"Who is it?" Marsha pressed. "That writer? Nathanial Cutter?"

"How did you know that?" Chloe wriggled from her grasp.

"Give me a minute," Marsha said, darting from the room and returning with an armload of books. "These. You asked me to hunt down and send you a copy of everything he's ever written."

"Yes," Chloe said, sighing. "So I did. And you never sent them."

"It's next on my list of things to do," Marsha said, piling the books on Chloe's already overloaded desk. "How serious is it with this guy? You going back?"

Chloe dropped into the chair Marsha had vacated and let her head fall back against the seat. She had no good reason to go. Whatever had motivated Nat Cutter's strange behavior, it had nothing to do with Sara. And she had several very good reasons not to return. He'd threatened her, frightened her, put her sanity to the test on a regular basis and had her half crazy with desire just by his presence. He'd come *that* close to compromising her virtue and now that he knew she was a publicist, he'd probably shoot her on sight.

"Listen, if you care about this guy," Marsha was saying, her tone softening, "get back there and straighten things out. I'll cover for you here."

Care about him? Why should she care about him? And why couldn't she swallow? "No, I'm not going back."

"Kiddo," her partner chided, coming to sit on the arm of the chair, "I don't know what's going on with you, but I can see you're hurting. You've got that 'little girl lost' look in your eyes. Hey—" she patted Chloe's arm "—if you want to talk, I'm here to listen."

Chloe shook her head and tried to smile. "Not just yet. Thanks, though."

A look of concern lingered in Marsha's eyes, but she nodded. "Okay, you're the boss." She stood up, stretched and grinned. "Problems of the heart always make me hungry. How about an early lunch?"

"No, you go ahead, I—"

"I know," Marsha said, starting for the door, "you've got some thinking to do." She disappeared, then stuck her head back in the doorway just long enough to say, "By the way, Gordon Browne called this morning. He knew you were back in town and was asking lots of questions. Weird man," she commented, and disappeared again.

Gordon Browne? What was he up to? Add another item to the list of reasons not to return to Maine, Chloe thought, Gordon Browne, a.k.a. The Shadow. She might as well call him and get it over with. There was no reason to protect Cutter anymore, or even to mention his name under the circumstances. It was going to be damn awkward though, she realized, trying to explain to Browne why she'd never mentioned the man she saw on the estate fourteen years ago, but if it helped in any way to locate Sara...

She rose and walked to the desk, a dull ache welling in her chest as her eyes were drawn to the books piled there. The volume on top was half the size of the others. His poetry? she wondered, catching herself as her fingers touched the book jacket. Her heart began to beat faster. Leave it alone, she warned instinctively.

But she couldn't. Like a woman obsessed, she picked up the small book and began to leaf through it. The poems were so starkly personal, Chloe's fingers shook as she read one after another. A ferociously angry work about injustice made her gasp, and a poignant ballad about the loss of love brought tears to her eyes. These aren't words, she realized, this isn't even poetry, this is a man's psyche laid bare.

At the back of the book, a poem entitled "Innocence of Heart" drew her attention. Only four stanzas long, it concerned the inevitable losses and disillusionments a child experiences in the journey to adulthood. She read it slowly, and then her eyes returned to the title. Suddenly she remembered where she'd heard those three words before.

"Oh no," she breathed, staggering backward, her hand flying to her mouth. *"Oh, my God."*

Eight

Nat Cutter stood in the doorway of the motel room, one arm propped up against the doorjamb. He took a long drink from a glass half-full of Scotch and stared out at the encroaching dusk.

An unseen sea gull cried.

He glanced at the room next to his, empty now, dark. Staring at the liquor left in his glass, he set the tumbler on the table by the door and walked back into the clutter of his room. Wads of paper dotted the cracked linoleum, the discarded efforts of his attempts to write. He sat down at the portable Smith-Corona, leaned back in the dinette chair and focused on a blank sheet of paper. You're losing your touch, he told himself sarcastically. Killing off your characters in new and different ways used to be a snap.

The sea gull cried again, distant now, a plaintive sound.

It echoed in his mind. Shut up, he thought, pulling the paper from the typewriter, crumpling it in his fist. I had to get her out of here. She was about to blow everything wide open.

He sat forward in the chair, determined to leach the last traces of her from his nervous system. The room, the whole damn state of Maine, was alive with her. In his mind, he could still see her out on those bluffs, burning with fever, trembling, *barefoot*. What kind of obsession was driving her? She wasn't a reporter out to break a big story. Syd's conference had confirmed that. But a publicist? How the hell did that connect?

When no answer came, his mind flicked irresistibly to her soaked and breathless body after the storm. He'd been with plenty of women, sexy women, but he'd never seen anything so erotic as the way she'd stripped off that T-shirt, her arms above her head, hands tangled in wet material, breasts freed, trembling.

His fingers ached, remembering. He hadn't even touched her. Now, he never would.

Exhaling, he rolled a sheet of blank paper into the machine and forced himself to concentrate on the murder scene he had to finish. He'd already had his deadline extended once....

The sea gull's faint keen drifted in with the evening breeze, and through it he heard his own name, a whisper, "Cutter."

God, now he was hearing her voice. You're getting maudlin, Cutter, he warned.

"Nat, I—"

He whipped around and came out of the chair, knocking it over with a deafening crash.

She hovered in the doorway, a small book clutched in her hand. "I have to talk to you." Her voice shook, but her jaw was set like stone.

His eyes swept over her. She had on the same herring-bone suit she'd worn at the conference, but the blouse was unbuttoned at the neckline, the skirt wrinkled. Her hair was a tangle of flames. "Why did you come back?"

Her eyes veered up to his. "To tell you who I am."

"I know who you are."

"No...you don't. But you will when I've finished. You'll know everything. Why I followed you here five days ago, why I'm here now. And when I'm done—" her mouth drew taut "—I want the same from you."

"I told you once. I rarely give people what they want."

"This time you will."

His instincts told him to stop her while he still could. Get her out of here. Put her on a plane to New York, then call Syd and tell him to make damn sure she stayed there.

"Unless you're afraid to hear what I have to say. Is that it, Cutter?"

"Damn," he exhaled, turning away, slamming his open palm against the wall and leaning into it.

Chloe winced at the sound, but held her ground, calcu-lating the risk of entering the room. When he didn't turn around, she stepped inside and began, talking hurriedly to his bowed head. "Fourteen years ago, I lived in upstate New York with my stepfather and his daughter. She—my step-sister—disappeared one night and was never found. Her name is Sara Guthrie." Cutting off, hushed, she watched for a sign, some indication of recognition.

Cutter remained motionless.

She went on, unable to stop herself, spilling out the events from the beginning: Joshua's appearance at Northpointe, her own encounter with him on the bridge, Sara's disap-pearance, the police, the dogs, all of it.

She hesitated toward the end, wishing he'd move, say something. She'd prepared herself for a strong reaction, even an explosion, anything but this. "James Guthrie's been ill," she said. "He nearly died a few weeks ago, and now he wants to find his daughter and make amends. That's all he wants, Cutter. No retribution or legalities, just Sara. And that's why I'm here." Her fingers tightened around the book. "Because you look like... him."

He turned around slowly.

"Like Joshua," she said, the words catching in her throat.

She felt a wave of shock and confusion as Nat Cutter faced her full on. His features were immobile, his expression unreadable, etched in stone. For a moment, in the room's murky lamplight, he didn't even resemble Joshua. Disoriented, she felt like she was seeing this man for the first time.

He shook his head, slowly, and doubts piled up inside her. Syd Reinhardt, Harvard, Europe, *Elena*. She'd seen it in the papers—the evidence that he wasn't Joshua. She couldn't deny it, any of it, *but the book*. It was Cutter's book, but they were Joshua's words. How could that be unless— Her eyes glanced from the volume pressed between her whitened fingers to him. "You wrote this, didn't you?"

He considered it a moment. "Yeah, I'll take the blame."

"And this?" She leafed through the book with trembling fingers until she found the poem. "This poem—did you write it? 'Innocence of Heart'? Are those your words?"

He exhaled and nodded. "Yes, I wrote it, and yes, those are my words, but I can't claim they're very original, or even very good—"

"He said these words to me. *He* said them, don't you understand?" She searched his face, hating the desperate ache in her chest. "I was twelve years old and terrified. He carried me out of the forest. He whispered things, beautiful things, and then he said three words to me, *innocence of heart*." She looked away from his shaking head, her voice dropping to a rasp. "How could you have written this...unless you were him?"

A painful silence followed until his voice, gentler, filled it. "Any number of people could have written those words, Chloe. And probably have."

His huskiness made her look up. And then she saw it, the dull light in his eyes, like something tortured.

"What is it?"

He shook his head and turned away, raking a hand through his hair. "God, how I wish you'd never come back here." His voice lowered, taut. "Do you have any idea what havoc you're wreaking in my life? I don't know what the hell I'm doing anymore. I can't even write, that's how crazy—" He broke off abruptly, reining himself in. When he came around finally, he looked almost haggard.

Studying her, he grimaced as though he had finally reached some painful understanding. "You said his name like he was some kind of god. You loved him, didn't you?"

The book slipped from her fingers and clattered to the floor. "I was a young girl."

"Young girls can love."

The darkness gathering in his eyes threatened to draw off all her energy. "Yes," she said, barely able to speak. "I may have—"

"Why?"

"I don't know. For the same reason I couldn't tell the police about him. Because I'd lost everyone I loved. Because he said my name and touched me, and no one had done that in so long."

Her eyes welled with unshed tears, and through the blur of moisture she saw a look of near anguish cross his face. As she stared at him everything came together at once for Chloe, past and present, radiating through her in soft waves.

The final realization, when it came, felt oddly like freedom. "You're not him, are you?" She wasn't asking him, she knew.

He shut his eyes briefly, shook his head and exhaled. "I wish I could tell you what you want to hear."

"No, it's all right. It's easier this way." She picked the book up from the floor and gripped it so tightly against her chest that its edges cut into her fingers. "I'm sorry for all of this. I know I've caused you all kinds of grief. I should never have come back here."

His jaw flexed and hardened.

In the brief connection their eyes made, she saw what she'd done to this stormy, private man who'd only asked to be left alone. "I'm sorry," she said, her voice aching. "I'll get out of your life."

Nat watched her turn for the door, and the words that could stop her locked in his chest. A blunt force assaulted him, like the thrust of a dull knife through his ribs. *"Wait."*

She stopped on the threshold, her back to him.

"You and I," he grated softly. "We're killing each other, aren't we?"

She jerked around, tears sparkling in her eyes.

The sight of her mouth, sensual and trembling, made him seize up inside. He wanted her more than he'd ever wanted anyone, anything in his life. He knew he had to let her go, that anything else would be insanity, but the flush transforming her pale face to radiance extinguished all thought of consequences.

Her breasts trembled beneath her blouse. His hands curled, aching. Insanity.

He turned away, an oath on his breath.

Chloe pressed a hand against the edge of the table, steadying herself. She searched for words that might ease the tension. "Cutter, I know I should go, but—"

He glanced back, his eyes grazing her with such ferocity she felt faint. They flicked to her breasts and she started as though he'd touched her there. An alarm sparked her nerves; a sudden flush aroused her skin.

Seeing his hands close into fists and release, she knew he meant to throw her out. She also knew he wanted her, badly, enough to tighten his jaw muscles to bands.

It would be so easy to break his control, she realized. And God help her, so dangerous! But if she left now she would never see him again, never feel that dizzying rush when his lips touched hers. Never know what it could be like with a man, with this man.

He turned back to her, his dark torment stunning.

It had to be this man.

"I know I should leave," she told him brokenly, "but I can't. Do you understand? Do you?"

Silent, he moved toward her.

"Cutter," she whispered. "I'm frightened."

He reached her, and his hands, fingers splayed, found her throat. Her breath caught hard as she imagined what he might do, but his hands lay still, exquisitely still, as he bent toward her.

The sensation of his mouth touching hers drew a shattering response, like a crystal falling through space and exploding on impact. Through the chaos, she heard her own body's soft cries of longing. They penetrated her to the bone marrow. All she could do was whimper.

Nat's hands tightened reflexively on her throat. Hearing her sob, he pulled back, hesitating, his breath harsh against her face. "Chloe...do you know what you're doing? Are you sure?"

Her stricken features were agonizingly beautiful to him. Her eyes were huge with fear, her mouth slightly swollen from his kiss. He ran his thumb along her jawline, then followed its path with his fingers. "Shall I stop?"

A moment passed while he caressed her, experiencing the textured silk of her skin beneath his unsteady fingertips.

Her eyes never left him and gradually the sensual flush returned to her face. He felt his heart surge as she began to shake her head. "No," she said, rising on her tiptoes, pressing her mouth to his. "Don't stop."

The excruciating softness of her drove him wild with longing. He slid his hand to the back of her neck, worked his fingers into her hair and without thinking closed his fist possessively.

The movement jerked her head back, and her startled cry sent his heart rocketing with excitement. Like a trainer with a frightened, unpredictable animal, he knew he had to slow down, gentle her. But the wild green pulse in her eyes devastated his control. God, she was *irresistible*.

His groin tightened painfully. Taking hold of her hips, he urged her into the fit of his thighs. As she softened against his hardness, another gasp, like a sharply drawn-in breath, shook her.

An urgent grace seemed to control her movements as she looked up and met his eyes. Her fingers touched his face, everywhere, more unsteady with each new discovery, and he felt a wrench of emotion that went beyond desire, beyond passion. I need her, he realized savagely. Like fire needs oxygen, I need her to survive.

Picking her up in his arms, he swung around, kicked the door shut and carried her to the bed.

Chloe felt an uncontrollable tremor of excitement as he began to unbutton her blouse. She'd never been undressed by a man before, and every brush of his fingertips against her skin made her heart quicken painfully. This was all new to her, this breathtaking intensity. His knuckles grazed her breasts repeatedly, each touch eliciting sensations that threatened to engulf her.

She reached up as though to stop him, but he caught her hand and turned it over, kissing her palm. "I know," he said, his breath flooding her skin, "I know." He met her eyes. "This is too fast for you, too new. We can take it slower if you want, *whatever you want*." The husky edge in his voice caressed her senses. "But if you're not ready, Chloe, if you can't go through with this, then say so now, before we're both beyond—"

"I can," she broke in, knowing it wasn't quite true. At his hesitation, she brought his fingers to her lips. "I am—ready." She felt him tremble and her heart surged.

He was swift and sure and stirringly gentle as he removed everything but her ivory satin slip.

Her inner world sharpened, honed with a new awareness as he paused to look at her. His magic still confounded her. He was a mesmerizing man…a spellbinder. But he was real. Not a fantasy, *real*.

His gaze stroked her body like radiant energy. Trembling, she felt the strap of her slip drop off her shoulder, seemingly of its own accord, and her breath came faster.

"If I could describe the way you look right now," he said, sitting opposite her, "I'd be a very rich poet."

He caressed her face and, at the same time, drew the remaining strap off her shoulder. As the satin fabric slid down her flushed skin, leaving her breasts naked, an exquisite shiver crossed her skin.

"You are devastating," he said, each word a groan from somewhere inside him.

His dark gaze brushed over her, stirring her nerves, tingling her breasts to taut, acutely sensitive peaks. Soft and swollen, they ached for the pressure of his hands. "Touch me, Cutter," she heard herself saying. "Now, please, *now*."

She caught his hand, and he pulled back. "Don't, Chloe," he warned. "You have no idea what you do to me when you say my name like that. I have to fight like hell not to take you—" He broke off, his jaw wrenching.

His admission startled and thrilled Chloe. She knew he was holding back, and for some crazy reason, she re-experienced the desire to test his control. Dangerous, she thought, her heart racing, *playing with fire.* Still, she touched her fingers to his mouth, drawing them along his lips.

He grimaced, as though a physical pain had gone through him. "Chloe, don't."

"But I want you to take me," she whispered.

Her heart caught as he took hold of her arms, pressed her back into the pillows and drew the satin material down to her waist. He loomed over her, the flash of his eyes blinding. Swept with lightheadedness, she felt his hands on her rib cage, moving with a crescendo of sensation to her breasts. "My God," she gasped, as instinctively frightened as a child caught in the ocean's undertow, *"Wait."*

She felt her senses dissolving into chaos under the sweet roughness of his hands.

A low moan vibrated through him. He caught her by the waist, accentuating the arch of her body, his lips searing her skin. She felt every breath of sensation, even the brush of his teeth as he took her breast in his mouth. Each urgent pull on her nipple aroused a knot of pleasure inside her. "Cutter," she whimpered, a sob in her throat.

His hands drugged her into a quivering, rapturous state of surrender. She felt the slip being dragged from her body and was helpless to stop him. Awash in an exquisite maelstrom of sensation, she heard herself sobbing softly, *"Wait."*

His body shuddered in response, startling her into consciousness. He brought her up by the shoulders, holding her face, raining kisses over her eyes and mouth. "God, I'm sorry," he said. "I'm insane. I'm scaring you half to death."

She gasped softly as he released her, her body quaking, alive with the traces of his mouth and fingers. "No, *no*, I'm not frightened. Cutter," she said, her voice a soft throb as she caught at his shirt, "please, it's all right."

"You're sure?" he said, and as she nodded, he put her hands away, stood up and pulled the shirt off over his head, throwing it aside. Body hair graced his tanned skin in the most sensual pattern she'd ever witnessed. As he unsnapped his jeans, revealing a dark, strategic arrow of hair, she felt a soft throb between her legs.

His pants dropped to the floor, and she looked away, stunned by the sight of him. She knew how men were built, but she hadn't expected— A flush stung her cheeks, and the knot of pleasure in her belly evaporated in fear. And then he was next to her, murmuring words so low and urgent she couldn't distinguish them.

After a moment he caught her chin and brought it around. "Is something wrong?" he asked. She shook her head, but couldn't stop herself from glancing down. His eyes followed hers, and he exhaled a short gust of laughter.

She tried to laugh, too, over the lump in her throat.

His jaw twisted. "Chloe, you know I'll have to hurt you a little."

The tenderness in his voice roused her heart to a deeper beat. She met his eyes and it was like staring into the sun. Yes, he might hurt her, she thought, but her body was already anticipating ecstasy.

She lay across the bed, and he came into her arms with a low groan, gathering her up and whispering kisses over her eyes and cheeks.

When he stretched alongside her, the feel of his body drenched her in sweet desire. He was hard and long and everywhere so gloriously warm.

"I don't care about the pain," she said, running her fingers over the muscles in his shoulders, "I want you, Cutter, *I do want you.*"

"Easy," he warned, catching her wrist, holding it still. "I'm trying my damndest to stay sane, but if you keep touching me like that, *talking* like that."

"All of you," she murmured wickedly.

"*Don't*, Chloe." He covered her mouth with a kiss and then rose over her. "Don't say anything more." His eyes glinted, stunning her with their darkness.

Again the contact of his body drugged her. His arms were hard and muscled. His hands were ruthlessly sensual as they stroked her nakedness, caressing her breasts with urgent pressure, purling softly across her belly. He touched the mounded triangle, and her body gave out an answering flash.

Soft moans swirled around her. Vaguely aware that they were her own, she felt him opening her legs, trailing his fingers up her innner thigh toward the quickening throb.

She cried out, and he gentled her with murmurs and hushes, caressing her with gradually increasing strokes of intimacy, priming her body slowly, stirring her nerves and senses to a state of sweet torment.

Dazed by the stimulation arcing through her, she pressed against him, only vaguely aware that he'd shifted his weight over her and eased his hips into the juncture of her thighs.

She felt him at the entry to her softness, and she was instantly alert. Her legs closed instinctively, but it was there, as hard as steel, a threatening physical presence lodged against her.

"I need you," he said, drawing her head up. The dark haunted beauty in his face stole the breath from her body. "Do you understand how much? I can't stop now, Chloe. Don't ask me to stop now."

The grip in his voice filled her with wonder and a desperate ache that crowded her heart. A sudden welling of emotion made her reach up to touch his mouth.

"Need me back, Chloe," he whispered against her fingers. "Take me inside you."

A radiance flared up from deep inside her. She arched against him, her fingers digging into his back. The first jolt of penetration brought a choked cry of pleasure.

"Am I hurting you?" he asked.

Amazed by the sweet, aching pressure of his body as it merged with hers, she could only shake her head. He hesitated halfway, gathering her tightly to him, and then with one quick stab of pain, he thrust deep inside her, filling her. The sudden and total union sent a wild cry of pleasure reverberating through her senses.

Inexplicably then, he stilled. She urged him to move with her hands and felt a thrilling quiver deep inside her. His whole body tautened. "Not yet," he said, holding her face with his hands. "When your body is used to the feel of me . . . then I'll move."

He kissed her lips, and she melted around him like warmed wine. In the hot flush of surrender, her body accommodated all of him. "God," he breathed, features contorting with strain. Easing back, he pressed into her again, losing himself in her warmth.

Her softness was too much for him; her heat seared his blood. He began to rock faster, deeper. A soft cry of pleasure came from her, mingling with his, as a brilliant rhythm built.

Their bodies knew each other; their bodies were destined.

Whispers filled the room, erotic, calling from beyond time, from the mists...an enchanter, a temptress who takes men's souls...

Again and again he buried himself inside her and felt his whole body drowning in sweetness. He tried to slow the mindless climb toward ecstasy and failed. The woman beneath him was torment; she was heaven. Her body was a silky glove, holding him in the exquisite grip of a woman aroused.

Moving, thrusting, surging with uncontrollable need, he acknowledged her broken gasps with caresses. She was trying to tell him what strange and wonderful things were happening to her. And then her body fluttered and tightened, and a sensation flicked through him like a whip crack.

She was climaxing and the knowledge snapped the last thin thread of his control. He pushed high into the narrow vault of her, shuddering as the light burst from him in a hot explosion. "No," he rasped, gathering her to him, crushing her in his arms. *"No."*

Someone whispered his name, sweet and shivery as bells.

"Chloe," he said, lost in sensation.

The light burst again, wondrous, and he felt as though his soul was being drawn from his body.

Nine

___

Chloe woke first...to a world that was a dreamy haze of soft-focus images. Heavy-lidded and languid, she peeked out from under the mountainous folds of the patchwork quilt. Sunlight sprinkled the room, capturing and suspending free-floating particles in its rays like fairy dust.

She turned on her side, elbowing up to consider the man sleeping with his back to her. With his dark hair ruffled against the white pillowcase, he looked like an eighteenth-century ruffian.

His back to her? That troubled her for a moment. When had he turned away? The last she remembered before they'd drifted off, he'd had her pinned in a dreamy wrestling hold—his head nuzzled into the hollow of her neck, an arm across her breasts, his leg entwined with hers.

Watching his back move in rhythm with his breathing, she contemplated this man who'd introduced her to ecstasy. Her heart still hummed with the words he'd whispered—lyrical and eloquent, the stuff of which fantasies are made.

All said in the heat of passion, she reminded herself, sobering. He'd been caught off guard last night. And this was the proverbial morning after. He might not feel so eloquent in the cold light of day.

As he shifted and stretched, dragging the covers farther down his back, Chloe's thoughts took an abrupt turn toward the physical. The wedge-shaped taper of shoulder to hip he'd exposed stirred an errant thought. Perhaps she'd just lift the blankets and take a peek at the rest of him.

Her heart beat a little faster as she argued against such silliness. A mature woman wouldn't, she thought, slipping a finger under the blankets and lifting. "Oh my," she breathed, her eyes straying to never-never land.

As though he'd heard, he swung around and rolled to his back. Chloe froze, her eyes darting to his face. Assured he was still asleep, she took another peek. "Oh *my*." She'd read an article about male hormones raging to their peak level in the morning. That author definitely knew her subject.

He opened his eyes. Chloe dropped the blanket.

"Lost something?" he inquired, a sleepy grin on his face.

"Just my mind." She was considering hiding under the covers for several hours, maybe the rest of her life, but then she'd be face-to-face with those hormones!

His smile deepened. "You're spectacular when you blush," he said, reaching up to caress her cheek. "Like a bowl of strawberries and cream."

She breathed a sigh of relief. He was still eloquent.

"You're pretty spectacular, too," she admitted, feeling the color deepen and tingle across her skin.

"Oh lady," he said, pulling her down beside him. "Don't make me lose my head again."

She snuggled into the muscular warmth of him, careful where she put her hands. "Why not? Then there'd be two of us."

Rolling to his side, his gaze intent on her features, he drew her into the circle of his arms. She sensed the passion in him, felt it in his aroused body. "I had a dream about you," he said.

His voice caressed her. It was tender and rough, the soft scratch of wool across sensitive skin. He didn't have to tell her what the dream was about.

An impulse, sweet and wicked, stirred her. Her hands whispered down to touch that forbidden part of him. "Want to make it come true?" The look in his eyes as she touched him sent the blood rushing and tumbling in her veins.

"Yes," he said, his face tautening. Foregoing the preliminaries, he lifted her leg and drew it up over his hip.

The abruptness of it all thrilled her. His hardness found its target, and her stomach spasmed with excitement. "In a hurry, Cutter?" she breathed, feigning nonchalance.

He caught her hips, his fingers biting into the soft flesh of her buttocks, and drew her down onto him. *"Yes,"* he said, a half smile flickering. "And under the circumstances, maybe you'd better call me Nat."

She let out a soft shriek of excitement as he simultaneously thrust up and eased her down. The tingling blush that had started earlier spread like wildfire, scorching her entire body. "Oh, yes, Nat," she gasped, melting around him just as she had the night before. *"Hurry."*

His swift strokes brought them to the peak of the mountain in moments. Chloe's body screamed for release and when it came, sudden and breathtaking, she felt as though she'd been flung off the summit and was free-falling to earth.

It was a long while afterward before she could rouse her
self. When she finally did, he awoke, too. Still entangled
their heads on the pillow, they stared into each other's eye
for a time before he managed a husky, "Good morning."

"You poet you," she said, unable to keep herself from
grinning like an imbecile. She'd never felt this wonderful—
she'd never been this happy in her life. It occurred to her
then, in a tiny, frightening explosion of insight, that she was
in love. Flat-out, fall-on-your-face in love. "Oh no," she
whimpered.

His face narrowed with concern. "Did I hurt you?"

No, but you will, she thought, anticipating the agony of
being hopelessly in love with such a man. She raised
shoulder in answer. "Just a twinge. I'm new at this, re
member."

An emotion she didn't understand whispered through his
features. With a slight shudder, he combed his fingers into
her hair and brought her face to his. "You're good for this
sinner's soul," he said, kissing her with such tender feroc
ity she felt her senses swim.

They came into each other's arms then, spontaneously
holding tight, neither quite understanding the other's ur
gency, and yet communicating with such intimacy through
the mute language of their bodies that they couldn't speak
when they parted.

The room grew silent, except for their breathing. Awk
ward and intense, they lay apart, fingertips touch
ing...until the silence was so painfully alive that Chloe had
to break it.

Gratefully, she remembered some unfinished business
"Speaking of souls," she said, her voice unsteady as she
drew back her hand and turned to stare at the ceiling, "what
about that Welsh myth? Gwydion and the woman made of

flowers?'' She lifted herself up on an elbow to look at him. ''You never told me the ending.''

Nat rolled his eyes. ''The elephants would kill for your memory.'' Sliding a hand from her waist to her breast, he cupped it and sent a warm shiver through her. His eyes told her that he wasn't interested in myths. The warm throb of his body told her exactly what he was interested in.

She held him off with a bawdy wink. ''Right after you tell me the ending.''

He tried his black magic on her—a penetrating look, a startling nip on her bare shoulder, but she, a thoroughly satisfied woman, wasn't having any of it.

''Okay then,'' he acquiesced, sitting up and bringing her with him. ''But first some coffee. I'm dangerous before my first cup.''

''Umm, now he tells me.'' Her stomach rumbled. ''And nourishment,'' she said. ''I'm starving.''

They dressed quickly, percolated coffee in a thin metal pot with a lid that didn't fit and found some stale doughnuts tucked away in a cupboard.

''A picnic,'' Chloe decided, grabbing a blanket and starting for the door. ''Come on,'' she coaxed. ''It's such a beautiful morning.'' Nat followed, grumbling, coffeepot and doughnuts in hand. While they were spreading out the blanket, the desk clerk appeared around the corner of the motel, gawked at them and shook his head before disappearing.

''What's with him?'' Chloe asked, smoothing the last lumps from the blanket before she sat down.

''Walt?'' Nat chuckled, joining her. ''I slip him some money and he makes sure I'm undisturbed. We writers need our sanctuary.''

''Walt—is that his name?'' She paused long enough to breathe in a long draft of sea air. ''Well, I hope you're pay-ing him enough because he's worth it. The man is inscrutable. I had to break into the office and steal a look at the registration book to find out that you were a registered guest here."

Nat looked at her curiously.

"On my honor." She raised a hand. "I couldn't pry a word out of the man."

"Really? Maybe I'll give him a bonus." He laughed, handing her a Styrofoam cup of coffee. "Now, do you want to hear the myth or don't you?"

She fished a doughnut out of the box and sank it into the steaming black brew. "I can't wait."

He took a gulp of coffee, grimaced and poured it out on the sand. "This stuff would strip paint."

Thinking better of eating her doughnut, Chloe set it and the coffee aside. "The myth," she prompted.

"It's not much of an ending," he admitted, scratching his forehead in a gesture that was almost sheepish. "Gwydion turned her into an owl."

"An *owl*?"

"Hold on," he said, "there's a certain poetic justice involved here. Gwydion created her from daylight and flowers, and he wanted an appropriate punishment. What could be more appropriate than a life of darkness?"

"But as an *owl*?" she complained. "It's just not—I don't know—romantic."

"Oh?" He surveyed her provocatively. "You thought it was going to be something sexy? Hoping for some debauchery, were you?" Catching her arm, he tugged her to him. "Come here, you little firebreather."

He chastened her with a "take that" kiss, whispered further kisses along her cheekbones and caught the tip of her chin off guard with a soft nip. "Sexy enough?"

He looked a little smug as they settled back to stare out at the ocean, so she murmured "For starters," and caught both her hands around his waist. Laying her cheek against his chest, she let the emotions run rampant inside her. Did every woman in love for the first time feel this way? Little flurries of excitement, the sweet ache of anticipation around the heart? Probably their stomachs didn't rumble, she thought, hearing hers. But other than hunger pangs, her immediate world felt like newborn bliss. Having no idea how long it might last, she savored it.

A blazing ball of sunshine spun heavenward, its ascent much too grand to signal just another morning making its debut. Not a cloud marred the blue sky. It's going to be a day of days, Chloe prophesied, drinking in a scene that seemed almost too beautiful to view.

After a time, Nat's hand ruffled her hair. "Chloe...I was married once."

Anxiety tapped at her. "I know. Syd told me, and I remember reading about it in the papers."

"Then you know how she died?"

"Yes." If he told her he was still in love with that woman, it would kill her.

"Maybe you should hear my version." He was quiet for a while, his chest rising and falling more noticeably. "I was just out of college," he said finally. "Full of ideas about truth and beauty—you know the type—a young turk out to right an off-center world. Elena was a beautiful, long-legged waif just begging for rescue. Nobody could talk me out of her, that's how sure I was that I could make a difference in her life."

He expelled some air. "Her death wasn't an accident. She killed herself over a part she didn't get. It was an absurd waste of life and beauty and talent, of everything that's meaningful."

"And you felt responsible?"

"I didn't love her. I thought I did, but afterward I realized that all I wanted was to save her. For the glory, I guess. I think she knew." He dropped his arms from around Chloe's shoulders and distanced himself a little. "No, I don't blame myself anymore."

But he did, she realized, and probably always would. "Would she have blamed you?"

He thought about that for a while. "She told me once she believed she was fated, pulled by some self-destructive siren's call."

"Sounds dramatic," Chloe observed, trying to keep her voice casual. Was it possible, she wondered, that Elena had unconsciously used Nat in some way—a self-fulfilling prophecy? "Maybe she didn't want to be saved," she suggested quietly. "Maybe that wasn't the role she auditioned you for...."

His head came around slowly. "What is this, no-wait psychoanalysis? Is there a bill in the mail?"

"Umm, at several times the going rate. I'm quick, but I'm expensive."

"Really?" His eyes twinkled, dark memories apparently set aside. He ran his thumb along the base of her throat and looked point-blank into her eyes. "How much?"

She felt a delicious flutter in her stomach. "For you? A repeat customer?" She could hardly believe the provocative things that came to mind. "Depends on what you need. Talk therapy has its moments, but in your case, I think some behavior modification—"

He emitted a throaty chuckle. "Behavior modification? Sounds rigorous." A glance at his watch sobered him. He looked up, apologetic. "I'm going to have to take a rain check. I've got an appointment with Syd and my publisher this afternoon."

"Today?" She caught at his arm.

"What's wrong?"

She shook her head, shivering as he put a hand to her forehead. "Are you running a temperature?" he asked.

"No, I'm all right. How long will you be gone?"

Rising, he helped her to her feet. "I'll cut it short and get a flight back tonight if I can."

"I'm going, too."

"No way, lady." His hand at her elbow, he urged her toward the room. "The only place you're going is to bed with two aspirin. You've been flirting with pneumonia since that morning we got caught in the rain."

She protested all the way to the four-poster, but his solicitous concern eventually won over her unease. She knew she didn't want him to leave, but no reasons came, just premonitions so vague and free-floating she couldn't express them.

He seemed to guess what she couldn't say, and in his reassuring ministrations, she glimpsed another side of Nat Cutter, unselfish and gentle—the man who rescued waifs and painlessly removed splinters from wounded hands. Propped up by pillows and feeling very much the pampered princess, she watched him throw some things together.

As he started for the door, a feeling of fear caught at her. "Wait, Nat, I'm better." She felt her head. "See, warm, not hot. And I need to go back anyway, to see Marsha. Business," she added emphatically.

He blew her a kiss from the door. "You'd have to hang on to the wing. I'm taking the shuttle and the flight's booked solid." Sun flooded the room when he opened the door. Squinting, he shaded his eyes with his hands. "Why didn't I pick up some sunglasses?"

Chloe threw back the covers. She knew those Carreras would come in handy. Her purse lay at the bottom of the bed. She found the sunglasses exactly where she'd been keeping them, in the zippered compartment. "Will these do?"

Nat's brows lifted in amazement. "How'd you—"

She thought about how she'd almost killed herself, hanging out over the ocean by a splintered railing. If she'd been one ounce heavier... She shrugged. "Piece of cake, actually."

At his laughing admiration, she allowed herself a momentary puff of pride, but she held the glasses back as he reached for them.

"Chloe, I'm in a hurry."

She took them with her under the quilt, shaking her head as he approached the bed. "I want you to come back, Cutter, whatever it takes. I don't know why these glasses are so important to you, but I'm hanging on to them until—"

A slightly exasperated grin adorned his gorgeous face. "I'll be back, lady, but not for the glasses." Scrutinizing her, he said, "But you don't believe that, do you?"

"Sure I do." Her fingers tightened on the metal frames.

"Trust me. I'm coming back." He closed in, knelt and kissed her. "Rest, hear? Don't get out of this bed. Don't even answer the phone." Touching her face, he added, "But do wait up for me, okay? We have some things to talk about when I get back."

She watched him open the door and stride into the sunshine, his words lingering in the air.

"Things to talk about?" she murmured. "Does that sound promising, or does that sound *promising*?"

She set the Carreras on the bedside table and rolled over to his pillow. Snuggling her head in the imprint, she luxuriated in the traces of him...remembered scents, sounds and textures. Nat Cutter was wildly sexy and impossibly difficult. Not a safe or sane choice for any woman. But he was her first man, her first love. She closed her eyes and smiled, triumphant. Nothing could change that.

Chloe's promise not to set foot out of bed held until noon. The day was glorious, her spirits high. And she'd seen almost nothing of the Pine Tree State of Maine except the four walls of the Sunrise motel.

Ignoring a pang of guilt, she dressed hurriedly. She'd go for a walk, or better yet, take the rental Datsun out for a spin, all the windows down. Maybe she'd drive up the coast.

Another place lingered in the back of her mind: White Rock Island. No, she thought, squinting as she opened the door, no more sneaking around behind Nat's back. She slipped on his way-too-large sunglasses and started for the car. I'll ask him about the island when he gets back. "We'll talk," she murmured aloud, *"intimately."*

The breathtaking drive up Route 1 conspired against serious thinking. Euphoric, Chloe dispatched her remaining concerns one by one with almost ruthless ease. *Sara:* Well, there was little else Chloe could do about her stepsister now except call Gordon Browne and tell him what she knew. *Joshua:* A memory, still poignant, yet oddly neutral. *The new Nat versus the old Nat:* Chloe looked at herself in the rearview mirror and winked. Never underestimate the curative powers of a good woman.

Her drive took her through several small, clustered communities before she reached Belmont, the first major coastal harbor. She might have continued on to Camden had she not noticed the large white clapboard house alongside the road. "The Midcoast Historical Society?" she murmured, pulling in.

She spent a half hour atoning for her history buff lie by browsing through artifacts dating back to the earliest settlements of the area. Steeped in New England pioneer heritage, she walked to the nearby harbor on foot, taking in the industrial seaport's architecture—austere, but somehow reassuring—and its locals, purposeful merchants and fishermen who seemed slightly startled when she smiled.

She had lunch on the waterfront, staving off starvation with half a Maine lobster and lots of crusty French bread. Afterward, she wandered at whim, perusing local shops and seashore museums along the city's main street, her senses pleasantly attuned to the briny smells and the noisy hiss and chug of the working harbor.

Coming out of a gift shop, she noticed the Belmont ferry pulling into its slip. A short line of cars and people waited to board. With rising interest, she realized it must be the shuttle that ran between Belmont and White Rock.

On impulse, she walked to the terminal, entered, approached the ticket counter and inquired about the ferry's schedule.

The clerk, a thin young man, began a painstaking recital of the entire day's schedule. "If you left now," he advised, summing up, "and caught the last ferry back at four-thirty, you'd have an hour and a half on the island."

"Thanks," Chloe said, mentally calculating. Adding on the hour's drive back to the motel, she figured she'd arrive somewhere between six and six-thirty. Nat hadn't said when he'd be back, but she was sure he'd be late, assuming he could arrange a return flight at all.

The clerk was regarding her expectantly. She glanced out the window at the boarding passengers and was sorely tempted. "Not today," she said finally. "Thanks anyway."

Her conviction a little shaky, she made for the door quickly, barely aware of the woman and adolescent boy who entered as she left.

Chloe was a quarter-block up the street when the ferry's horn sounded, a mournful blast that reverberated through her nerves. She turned around, her eyes drawn to the terminal as the woman and boy came out and hurried toward the boat.

Something about the woman struck her, the slender frame in motion, the cascade of white-gold hair. The ferry horn sounded again, a horrible wail. The woman said something to the boy and they began to run.

Perspiration sheened Chloe's forehead, her upper lip. No thoughts came to her whirring brain, just a constant jamming signal. She began to follow them, jerky, her legs surging and halting.

As they ran up the ramp, the ferry gave out one last howl, and the bulwarks closed behind them. Lurching forward unsteadily, Chloe felt a mute cry building.

A cluster of departing passengers blocked her path. She tried to avoid them, hit someone's shoulder and staggered.

"You're too late, miss," a man called as she reached the gate that spanned the road. "Next one leaves at two-thirty."

"I know," she said, watching the ferry pull away. Her hands froze on the railing as the woman turned around slowly to look back. The blond hair lifted and fluttered in the wind like corn silk. Her blue eyes caught light from the sun. She was the most beautiful woman Chloe had ever seen.

She was Sara Guthrie.

A low roar exploded in Chloe's head. Gripping the metal gate dizzily, she saw the boy join Sara at the railing. His dark hair and eyes were a direct contrast to Sara's fairness, and his adolescent features had that look of a young male in transition.

He looked directly at Chloe, and their eyes connected for an instant before he disappeared among the other passengers.

"No," she whispered, shaking her head, backing away. Her chest was a vise, cutting off her wind. Her legs felt weighted and trembling. *"His eyes. Dear God, he has Nat's eyes."*

Ten

The drive back to the Sunrise motel was a blind journey through time and space. Everything beyond the highway lane Chloe occupied spun away like refracted light and dissolved into pale streams. When she pulled into the motel parking lot, she had no idea whether she'd been on the road minutes or hours. The clock in the room told her it was nearly 5:00 p.m.

With her purse in her lap, she sat on the bed wondering why she was there, in his room, sitting on his bed...and why she felt nothing.

She looked around the room, her sense of detachment growing. None of it seemed real—last night's dreamlike intimacy, today's nightmare. The emptiness inside her felt as though it might expand until she disappeared. She touched her own face, her fingertips icy against her skin. If she could think, talk, she could fight off the numbing shock.

Ask yourself a question, she thought, any question. One gradually materialized. Why hadn't they condemned that old pier at the beach? Someone could be hurt there. Another question, quickly. Why can't we live without lies?

She stood up, her purse sliding to the floor, her voice hushed. "Is that where she's been hidden all this time? On the island with the boy?" Dark eyes flashed at her from a young curious face. "His son?"

She let out a broken sob and caught hold of the bedpost to steady herself. *Some things to talk about when I get back,* that's what he'd said. She'd thought he meant them, their relationship. Now she knew he was going to tell her about Sara and the boy.

She closed her eyes, her mind racing ahead of her with the ruthless efficiency of a machine fueled by pain. It was all beginning to make sense, his anguish the night before, his behavior since the beginning, the secrecy, the intimidation.

She'd told Nat everything, and now that he knew Sara had nothing to fear from Guthrie, he could make a clean breast of it. He'd undoubtedly planned to tell her when he got back from New York. And along with his confession, he'd explain why it was impossible for them to see each other again. Or maybe he'd want an affair? *Oh, God.* Her heart wavered, a painful hesitation. Her eyes came open. "No—he's not like that, not purposely cruel."

Another soft thud of awareness rocked her. He *is* Joshua. She dragged in a breath. *My* Joshua.

In the blur that followed, time reached out its unforgiving hand and swept her back. Rapid brush strokes painted the past in deep-stained hues of red and blue. Defenseless against the slashes of color, Chloe relived her losses—her mother, a father she'd barely known and Joshua—and felt again the heartache that only an abandoned child can feel.

Her jaw clenched, trembling. "Stop it," she whispered. "That was so long ago. Don't do this to yourself."

Drawing in a quick, fierce breath she bent to pick up her purse. Go home, she told herself brutally, leave the three of them to their life. You've done what you came to do, you've found Sara. Nat will tell her about her father. They'll be all right now...all of them.

She had the motel door half open when a rattling burst of sound stopped her. The telephone. Her body froze; her heartbeat accelerated. She prayed the phone would stop ringing, and then, afraid it had stopped, she rushed to pick it up.

"Chloe?" Nat's voice called. "Is that you? How's the patient?"

Mercifully, a spray of static cut him off.

"Are you there?" he asked. "We've got a bad connection."

"Yes, I'm h—" Her throat convulsed, swallowing the words.

"I can't hear you. Let me call you back," he suggested. *"No."*

"Okay, then listen to me, Chloe. I can't get back tonight. Syd's got a big deal cooking, several books, and he wants me to stick around until tomorrow to finalize it—"

As she listened to him describe the seven-figure contract Syd was negotiating, an impulse moved through her, a wrenching need to cut through the impersonal conversation and silence him with the truth. He'd hurt her, God, how he'd hurt her. How could he talk about finalizing deals and contracts? How could he be so casual when he knew he was coming back to tell her about Sara? And if he was going to tell her the truth anyway, why not last night? *Before they had made love?* Hurt swelled to outrage. *Explain yourself,* she wanted to shout at him.

"Wish I could get back there tonight," he added over the crackling on the line, "but Syd's wound up like a clock spring. Will you be okay?"

Chloe couldn't hear what he'd said over the sharp surge of her heart, but a word, *a name,* spun out at her. *Syd.* Her brain made the connection with a chaotic pop of awareness. Syd, Harvard, Elena. Nat had been married. He'd told her himself. But all those years in Europe. But how could that be? Sara— Confusion swept her.

"Chloe, what's wrong?"

The certainty she'd felt earlier became hazed with doubt. An instinct silenced her. There was something going on here she didn't understand at all.

"Chloe, dammit, talk to me. Are you sick? Do you need a doctor?"

"No, I'm fine," she said slowly, her thought processes beginning to clear. The shock of seeing Sara and the boy had blocked out all conflicting information. The connection had been instant—Nat, Sara, their son. But now she didn't know. There were so many inconsistencies—

"You're not fine. I can hear it in your voice."

His intensity stirred her, but she couldn't give in to it. The possibility that he'd lied to her made everything he'd said, and would say, suspect. Somewhere—was it in her mind?— she heard the faint blast of a departing ferry.

"I am, really," she told him, forcing energy into her voice. If she could get to Sara . . . her stepsister might have the answers. "I'm taking it easy here, a good rest, so relax and take your time. Don't worry about me, *promise*?"

"Okay." He sounded perplexed. "See you tomorrow then."

"Yes."

Neither hung up. "Nat—" Breaking off, she found it almost impossible to speak. "Good luck with the deal."

"Thanks," he said. "And hey, firebreather...I miss you."

She closed her eyes, swallowed painfully and without a sound replaced the receiver. Fumbling for her purse, she anticipated the telephone's next eruption and shuddered when it didn't come.

She couldn't tell him what she was going to do because he might try to stop her. Her chest tightened with conflicting emotions. She had to get out of the room in case he called back. She had to get out of the area in case he *came* back.

Within minutes, she was pulling the rental Datsun out onto Route 1 toward Belmont. Dusk was descending, already dominating the sky. She shivered and switched on the headlights, wondering where she would stay that night.

Think, she ordered silently. Did she have enough gas to make it? Would it rain tonight? Her foot pressed the gas pedal. What was the speed limit? Think, think about what's coming around the next bend in this road. Think about the ferry, the island, Sara.

Intuition told her Sara was the source. With each passing mile, she felt more certain that getting to Sara meant understanding everything.

An energy drove Chloe, but she knew better than to completely trust its momentum. Her instincts were too skewed with emotion. She'd been sure before—and burned each time.

But the energy was there, undeniably. And with it came fear. A resurgence of the premonition, however irrational, that someone didn't want her to get to her stepsister.

In the next half hour, she decided against a motel. She didn't like the idea of registering—even with a false name—or the dread of sitting and waiting. She felt safer with the car's potential for motion and power. But if she stayed in the car, she had to find a place to park. The police would notice her in Belmont, even on a side street.

Twenty minutes from the city, she pulled off Route 1 onto a deserted dirt road and parked alongside a sheltering copse of trees. Assuring herself that she couldn't be seen by passing cars, she settled back, shut her eyes and resolved to wait out the night.

Chloe's eyes blinked open. Momentarily disoriented, she sprang up, grazing her thigh on the steering wheel. The first light of dawn filtered through the trees. It was morning. She fell back in the seat and let out a sigh of relief, her worst fear averted. She'd made it through the night. There'd been other fears, born in the darkness, plenty of them. But it was morning now, *daylight*, and she'd survived them all.

The business of getting to Belmont and the ferry terminal preoccupied her. She had an hour if she started now, plenty of time. A quick twist of the ignition key brought the Datsun awake, eliminating another fear.

Back on the road, she considered stopping at a gas station to clean up and decided in favor of the ferry's rest room. She hadn't changed her clothes since Syd's conference, and her slept-in herringbone suit looked it.

A shudder shook her, and then another one, violent. Startled, she realized she was chilled to the bone. She turned the heater on high, and by the time she reached Belmont she felt as though her blood had begun to circulate normally again.

A sign at the entrance to the ferry terminal parking lot clearly stated that only island residents were allowed cars on the island. The parking lot provided little cover, but Chloe weighed her options and decided an empty corner space with an unobstructed view of the ferry was worth the risk. At least from where she sat she could watch the passengers' comings and goings, and then, at the last minute, buy her ticket and board. It seemed crazy in the clear light of day to be calculating her every move, but she couldn't dismiss the lurking conviction that someone might not want her to find Sara. Possibilities ran through her mind: Nat, Gordon Browne, or someone else unknown to her?

The blast of the ferry's horn jarred her into action. She locked the car hastily and hurried to the terminal. The same clerk helped her, with the same methodical efficiency, and if he was surprised to see her again, he concealed it well.

An excruciatingly long wait in the boarding line increased Chloe's agitation. She glanced over her shoulder repeatedly, and when the attendant finally opened the gate and waved the passengers aboard, she glanced back one last time—into the curious eyes of the people lined up behind her. You're acting like an escapee from somewhere, she warned herself. Stop searching people's faces and calm down.

She found the rest room before they even pulled away from the slip. The cold tap water shocked her senses. Braving its icy bite, she washed her face vigorously, then put on some fresh makeup and brushed her hair.

By the time she emerged, most of the passengers had taken seats in the ferry's small cabin enclosure. She walked the outer deck instead, thinking, planning her search.

The thirty-minute crossing went quickly, too quickly for Chloe as she stood at the railing and watched White Rock's looming silhouette take form. Something about the island's water-bound isolation reminded her of a prison. Was Sara happy there? Was she there of her own will?

Coming from nowhere, the second question jarred Chloe, but she found herself unable to put it aside. Sara wasn't physically imprisoned, of course, because Chloe'd seen her and the boy returning to the island yesterday. But there were other ways to control people, psychological constraints like dependency, intimidation, and even—Chloe's heartbeat quickened . . . sexuality.

Her mind flashed instantly to Nat Cutter and his effect on her. Such a stark, mesmerizing presence, enough to frighten off any woman, and yet, in just a few days' time, Chloe had surrendered it all to him, everything she held precious, her body, her heart. She caught in a breath, remembering.

She couldn't explain why she'd responded to him in ways she'd never responded to any other man. But Cutter was no ordinary man. Just his voice alone could thrill her into mindlessness. And beyond that, it was something to do with his eyes. Uncanny. They had a hypnotic quality, those eyes, beautiful . . . and terrible.

Chloe could almost believe he had some kind of hold on Sara. She could almost believe he was the reason Sara hadn't contacted her father in fourteen years.

A low wailing blast jarred her. She grabbed the rail, her heart racing. Easy, she told herself, it's just the ferry. Feeling the boat slow as it pulled into the dock, she walked along with the other passengers to the exit ramp.

The island was beautiful, rocky and green, and, at first glance, primitive. She saw a few concessions to civilization as she descended the ramp: paved streets, telephone poles and several homes with the rustic weather-beaten charm of Cape Cod cottages.

Looking around the quiet harbor, disproportionately populated with sailboats, she realized she had no idea where to start. The exit road from the ferry branched off in several directions, but most of the cars were turning left at the intersection and heading up a slight incline. Follow the crowd, she thought.

The hill descended into a small village of stores and shops, a real-estate office, a garage and a rambling unnamed block building that had the official look of a town hall. Chloe launched her search at a one-room mom and pop grocery store with a rusty porch swing out front.

Confident that it shouldn't take too long to find a woman who looked as Sara did, she gave the proprietor a cursory description and was surprised when he took his pipe out of his mouth just long enough to say, "Sorry. Can't help ya."

"But you must have seen her," Chloe pressed. "Her name is Sara, and she's in her early thirties." Chloe hadn't planned to say anything more, but now she felt compelled. "There was a boy with her, around thirteen or fourteen, dark hair."

"Nope, don't know either of 'em," he said, pleasantly enough. "Something else I can do for you?" The calm finality in his manner discouraged further questions.

"Yes." Realizing she was starving, she picked up some cheese, hard French rolls and an apple, paid for them and left. When you're starving everything's delicious, she thought, devouring the apple first as she considered the real-estate office across the street. "And when you're looking for something," she observed, remembering a stock line of her mother's, "you can never find it."

She was halfway across the street when she heard a buzzing sound. She glanced around, saw nothing and continued walking, but the drone persisted, swelling into a whining high-pitched roar. Down the street to her left, a bright blue blur wheeled off a side street and bore down on her.

Chloe dashed for the stoop of the real-estate office, reached it and whirled around just as something that looked like a streamlined golf cart pulled its shuddering bulk and full-blown racket up alongside her. Its driver, a husky blue-eyed teenager, grinned at her. "Delivering groceries," he volunteered, with no apologies for lopping ten years off her life. "You going all the way around the island?"

Panting like a winded animal, she nodded. And wondered how he knew.

"Long way. Want a ride?"

She considered the vibrating machine. "I think so. Give me a minute." After a steadying breath, she introduced herself, told him why she was on the island and described Sara.

"Never seen her." His eyes squinted thoughtfully. "And it'd be real hard to miss a lady like that. Sure she lives here?"

Hope plummeting, Chloe realized Sara might not be living on the island. She could have been visiting, sight-seeing, anything. The possibilities were endless and endlessly depressing, especially since they hadn't occurred to her before. "She was here yesterday," she said staunchly. "Someone must have seen her."

Behind the bravado, she knew she had no choice but to go on. The island was all she had. She climbed into the golf cart beside him. "I'll take that ride."

They looped the small island in just under two hours, including stops at the infrequent clustering of homes that dotted the shoreline. Not only did the islanders Chloe spoke to not know Sara, several of them began shaking their heads before she'd finished her stepsister's description. Others didn't even bother to answer their doors. Her mother's line was turning out to be prophetic, Chloe realized, as they chugged up the last hill and the village came into view.

Scanning the nearly deserted main street, she experienced one of those elusive premonitions that all is not right. She was tempted to explain away both the feeling and the aloof treatment she'd received with bromides like typical New England reticence. But another stirring was taking hold, the distinctly crazy feeling that she might be the victim of some kind of conspiracy of silence.

"Too bad you didn't find your friend," her young driver said as they pulled up in front of the general store.

"Yeah," she agreed. "Thanks anyway." Preoccupied with her thoughts, she got out of the cart and smiled at him. What would she do now?

"Maybe she lives on one of the other islands," he suggested, his shoulders lifting.

His answer came so quickly after her silent question it spooked her. This was the second time he'd anticipated her. "Other islands? On this ferry's route?" She didn't remember the clerk at the terminal mentioning other islands.

"Yeah," he said eagerly. "Well, just a couple more, but if you really need to find her, you'd better check 'em out."

Chloe felt her legs and her spirit buckling. The prospect of checking out even one more island overwhelmed her. She shook her head and then another thought occurred to her. "Are there any more homes in the interior of this island?" she inquired hopefully.

"Not . . . really." Pointing to his diver's watch, he added, "If you're going to catch that ferry, you don't have much time. Next one leaves in twenty minutes."

Chloe remembered the exit road from the ferry forking off in several directions. It seemed odd there'd be no homes on those roads. A hunch sparked as she glanced at his expectant face. He wanted her off this island. It was nearly as crazy as the conspiracy of silence idea, but she decided to play it out. "Twenty minutes? Then I'd better get going. Thanks again."

"S'okay," he said, beaming. "Hey—I'll drop you off at the slip."

"No," she said quickly. "I'd like the walk. Do me good." She waved and started off, hoping he didn't follow.

She remembered correctly. The intersection before the harbor forked out in three directions, including the road she'd returned on. The other two roads led into the island, and one of them had a wooden signpost with four surnames branded into the surface.

Chloe got the same response at all four houses, a disapproving look and a single syllable "Nope." On the way back, she noticed an overgrown driveway she'd missed, and tucked back in a dense thicket of trees, a rustic log cabin with an incongruously shiny boy's bike by the front door.

She knocked at the door and hesitated when no one answered, thinking she'd heard someone inside. "Anyone home?" she called, walking around to the back. From all angles the house appeared curtained and silent.

The ferry's horn sounded in the distance. Torn, Chloe circled the house again, knowing she had to catch the ferry if she wanted to make the other islands today. The boat's second wail tugged at her. She broke away, reached the road and began to run the last two hundred or so feet to the intersection. Her strapped, low-heeled shoes slapped against pitted, water-warped pavement.

The attendant saw her as she darted across the empty intersection. "Come on, miss," he called, waving her on.

Breathing heavily, she reached the ramp, climbed it and nearly collided with the man's outstretched arm. "Ticket, miss."

"Oh, yes." Shuddering through the ferry's next blast, she searched her purse, found the ticket and boarded. The gate closed behind her, and the ferry's engines roared in preparation to pull away.

Turning back to look at the island, Chloe formulated a last-ditch question and yelled at the attendant over the din. "Did you notice a blond woman and a dark-haired boy on this ferry yesterday?"

He nodded, and Chloe slumped against the railing. "Where did they go? Which island?"

"Only one island on this route," he told her shrugging. "This here one. Seen that blond lady before, I think. Must live on White Rock somewhere."

"Let me off," she said. The ferry lurched. "Let me off now!"

He opened the gate, and Chloe descended the ramp, stepping off just as it lifted away from the boat. The last house, she thought, it has to be that one. Half running, half stumbling, she retraced her steps to the log cabin.

She avoided the driveway, skirting the crescent of trees and approaching from the side instead. She didn't want to alert whoever might be inside.

Crouched beneath a curtained window, she listened, and after several moments of silence, slipped around to the back of the cabin. Pressing in close, she stopped, her heart jerking. The cabin's back door hung open a crack.

A twig snapped beneath her foot as she stepped forward. Everywhere, sounds magnified. Murmurous breezes rustled the trees, and a dog barked several times and stopped abruptly. The door creaked on its hinges. Chloe shrank back, her heart hammering. The wind?

An uneasy silence resumed. She edged closer, listening at the narrow opening. An empty house sounds different, she thought, no residual traces of human activity, not even the rhythmic breathing of someone asleep.

She entered the darkened kitchen, surprisingly modern for a cabin, and crept noiselessly across shiny vinyl tiles.

It was the flickering shadow at the end of the hallway that caused her to freeze. She stepped back, pressing into a closed doorway. Someone was in the house. Groping for the doorknob behind her, she felt it twist beneath her fingers. In the same instant the door jerked open, and she fell screaming into the room.

A man's hand caught her arm and pulled her to her feet. Twisting, she got a glimpse of his shadowed face before his arm locked around her neck. "*Nat*, why—?"

A damp rag smothered her cry. She inhaled instinctively, dragging the acrid odor of chloroform deep into her lungs.

Eleven

Consciousness came slowly, a glimmer in the murky well of Chloe's mind that expanded until it was a light beneath her eyelids. She saw a coffee table first and then the far arm of a couch and a woman's outstretched legs, oddly bent and half hanging off the cushions. *My own legs,* she realized as the haze began to clear. A dimly lit room swayed around her.

She tried to think through the dull throb in her temples, but the partial images floating in her mind wouldn't jell...a dog's bark, an open door, a man. It all seemed so recent, so urgent.

Struggling to sit up, she saw him. He stood at the window, his back to her, holding the curtain open just enough to look out. *Nat?*

Her foot snagged the coffee table, and the unexpected contact set off a wave of nausea. Swaying weakly, she fought down the sensation. When she looked up he'd dropped the curtain and was turning around, his body a black outline against the diffuse sunlight penetrating the curtain.

Seeing him brought it back, the struggle, the drop into blackness. She felt panic but she couldn't find any words.

He shifted in the shadows. "Cutter," she whispered as he walked toward her. "Why?"

He paused in a stream of light from the hallway, and she saw his face. The dark features were strikingly familiar, and yet they collided with the image of Nat Cutter in her mind. This man was tall, lean, dark-haired, but his features... She strained to see facial contours that lacked the angular definition she remembered, a mouth less carved.

The light was fuzzy, her senses still disoriented from the drug. She must be imagining the subtle differences. He moved closer, in and out of the shadows, and for a second she felt as if she were trapped in a house of flashing mirrors, turning, blinking—everywhere she looked another image of Nat Cutter, all different, yet the same.

It was his eyes that halted the whirl. Her disorientation vanished as he hesitated at the edge of the coffee table, close enough for her to see detail, even color. *Hazel eyes, flecked with green.* "You're not—" She pressed back into the couch. *"Who are you?"*

The edge of his mouth curled, hostile. "Who sent you here?"

The voice could have been Nat's, even the inflection. The suspicion surging in his question took her back to that first morning in Nat's room. Even then she'd had the premonition that Nat Cutter was two men. She'd been thinking in terms of psychological complexity, one man with two disparate personalities. But now, as she stared at his eerie replica—

"Who sent you here?" he repeated.

"No one."

"I want the truth," he snapped. "You've been harrassing my neighbors. You broke into my house. Why?"

"Who are you?" she whispered.

"Dammit—" He kicked the table aside and lunged forward to grab her arm. "Answer the question."

Chloe's started cry brought a gasp of alarm from the hallway. A woman appeared, blond hair flowing around her shoulders. "Let her go," she insisted, hovering. "You promised she wouldn't be hurt."

"I'm not going to hurt her." He released Chloe's arm. "I just want the truth."

Chloe stared at the woman, her breath caught in a mix of relief and awe. She was a wraith from the past, moving with the same grace and fragility Chloe remembered as she walked to the man poised by the coffee table and touched his arm.

"Sara?" Chloe murmured.

She turned, startled, staring at Chloe. "What did you call me?"

Chloe tried to stand, but the man's warning glare stopped her. "Sara, I'm Chloe," she said awkwardly. They'd never had a close relationship, rarely seen each other with Sara away at school, but she added without thinking, "Chloe— your sister."

Sara's face drained of color.

Instantly, Chloe regretted having said it. The flare of distrust in the man's eyes was terrifying. Sara tried to stop him, but he moved away from her grasp.

"Did James Guthrie send you?" he demanded.

"No," she said quickly. "I came on my own. No one knows I'm here."

His eyes bore into her, as though he was trying to penetrate to some vulnerable part of her and read the truth. He was so like Nat, she thought, a chill icing her skin. But her eyes were adjusting to the low light, her senses sharpening. This man's hair was a half-shade lighter, his skin tones ruddier, she realized. And the light in his eyes was fueled by a different source than Nat's. Survival. He had the hunted look of a man on the run.

A question sparked in her mind. *Is he Joshua?*

He glanced at the slender woman, and Chloe saw their silent exchange. The air breathed of tension, as though they were waiting for someone to appear. Quickly, Sara walked to the window, eased the curtain open and looked out.

He turned back to Chloe. "What do you want with her?"

"Her father—" She hesitated. "He's been ill."

"Guthrie?" He moved forward. "You said he didn't know you were here."

"He doesn't."

"Wait, Rob." Sara had turned from the window. "My father, ill? What do you mean?" She approached the couch with evident concern.

Rob? The name eddied in Chloe's mind, pooling and sliding over impenetrable surfaces like an incoming tide. Maybe Joshua didn't exist, maybe she'd only imagined him.

"Please, Chloe," Sara pressed, sitting next to her. "What's wrong with my father?"

"It was his heart. He's over the crisis now, but it was close." A hand touched her. Looking down, she focused on the pale skin and attenuated bones. Sara's hand. The sister she'd admired from a distance, wanted to know. She looked up. "Your father wants to see you, Sara."

"No—" Rob muttered in the background.

"Let her finish, Rob," Sara intervened. "Chloe, when did you talk to him?"

"In the hospital. It was about two weeks ago." At the light pressure of Sara's hand, she went on. "He was in intensive care when I saw him, and very ill, but he wanted to know if I'd heard from you—wouldn't let me leave until I convinced him I didn't know where you were. Afterward, his assistant told me how desperate he was to find you." She tried to smile and couldn't quite. "Your father wants to try to make up for whatever's happened between the two of you. He wants to start over."

"Sara," Rob warned, *"it's a trap."*

Chloe looked up at him, questioning the rancor in his voice. His eyes were fixed on Sara, full of anger, concern and an urgent kind of love. Was he the man at the bridge? she wondered. Confusion eddied again as she realized how much she still didn't understand. "Sara, what happened between you and your father. Why did you run away from Northpointe?"

Sara looked up at Rob, a question in her eyes.

"No," he said, shaking his head.

"But I want to tell her," Sara argued softly. "I'm sure we can trust her, Rob, please."

He walked to the window, looked out. "How can you trust anyone connected with him after what he's put you through?" He grasped the curtain, yanked it closed. "Put *us* through?"

She got up, went to him and after a few whispered words turned back to Chloe. "How did you know I was here? Someone must have told you I was on this island."

"No—no one. I was in Belmont yesterday. I saw you boarding the ferry." Quickly, Chloe relayed her own account of the incident at Northpointe, describing Joshua. "I saw him again, or thought I did, at a writers' conference in Cape Cod a few weeks ago, only his name was Nat Cutter. That was before I knew your father was ill, Sara. After the hospital visit I followed Cutter here, to Maine. I thought he might lead me to you."

Again, she saw them exchange looks. This time Rob nodded.

Sara walked to the couch. "You were right about Nat." She spoke slowly, as though she knew how important it was to Chloe. "He is the man you saw at the bridge. His name is Joshua Whitney, and he's Rob's older brother."

Chloe's throat tightened. She searched Rob's face. Of course, brothers. A poignancy she didn't quite understand brushed her heart.

Rob sighed. "Go ahead, tell her, Sara," he said gently. "Start at the beginning."

Sitting on the couch, staring beyond Chloe at some distant scene, Sara reopened the past reverently, like a cedar chest full of scented treasures. She and Rob had met in college, and the cliché, well, it was true in their case. Love at first sight, love at first breathless glimpse. They'd dated for over a year, but Sara kept it from her father. "He'd disapproved of every boy I'd ever mentioned, even casually," she said, her breath a sigh. "And Rob was too important. I couldn't take the chance that he'd order me not to see him again."

She stopped, staring down at her hands, as though she wanted to stay with those memories and not go on.

"I was happy," she said, a catch in her voice. "In a state bordering on bliss, really. And when I found out I was pregnant it seemed perfect, planned. I believed we were destined to be together, Rob and I. And the baby proved it."

Chloe saw tears sparkling in Sara's eyes and felt a sympathy build within her.

"We were going to run away," Sara said, brushing her cheek. "But my father found out. My father knew everything." She looked up at Rob, remembered pain moving in her features. "And he used everything he knew."

An emotion very near hatred burned in Rob's eyes as Sara went on.

"He sent Gordon Browne to the school to bring me home, and then had one of his men try to buy Rob off. When that didn't work, he resorted to threats. I didn't know until later—" her voice lowered "—that Rob was suspended from school on trumped-up charges and finally expelled."

Sara glanced back at the man by the window, and a wavery smile appeared. "I also didn't know about Rob's plan to rescue me. Sounds a bit Arthurian, doesn't it? Dragon slayers and maidens—"

Rob's voice sliced through Sara's attempt at lightness. "Guthrie told me he was sending Sara out of the country. He said he'd make sure I never saw her or the baby again. I tried everything, even talked to lawyers, but nobody would go up against him.

"Time was running out," he added grimly, "and I was desperate. I knew if I wanted Sara back, I'd have to go and get her myself, so I swiped a gun from my father's collection and got caught. Josh was due to leave for Europe, but my mother called him back, thinking he was the only one who could handle me...."

He means Nat, Chloe realized when the name registered a half beat later. It struck her as odd, since her intuition had once been so strong, that she now found it hard to fathom that Nat and Joshua were the same man.

Sara was talking, finishing the story in her soft, tremulous voice. "Rob convinced Josh to help him. They were two of a kind then, both idealistic and passionate about justice. I don't think it ever occurred to my father that Rob would have the courage to defy him, and he certainly hadn't counted on the formidable Whitney brothers." Her mouth quirked into a shy, charming smile. "The two of them whisked me right out from under his nose."

Rob grinned, and Chloe felt like applauding.

"Unfortunately," Sara continued, "my father doesn't take defeat lightly. We managed to evade his detectives for a while, but they caught up with us in California right after the baby was born. We were married by then and thought foolishly that there was nothing he could do." She stopped, a shadow crossing her face.

Chloe sat forward. "What happened?" She heard her own heart beating in the silence.

"He tried to take our son away from us," Sara said, raising her eyes to Chloe's. "He brought in a team of high-powered lawyers and sued us for custody. He claimed we were child abusers." She shook her head, looked away. "It wasn't true, but we knew he'd win. We had to run."

"You and Rob?"

"All three of us," Rob cut in. "We took the baby and went to Canada, and when they tracked us down, we flew to Europe. It's easier to disappear there. Josh and Elena lived in Italy, and with their financial help and contacts, we got lost—" he emitted a short, cold sound "—so lost even James Guthrie couldn't find us."

"But you came back," Chloe observed.

"Yeah, about a year ago. Josh had been here in the States for several years. When he was sure Sara's father had called off his dogs, he contacted us. He'd scouted the island, found this place." He shrugged as though he felt the need to defend his decision. "We wanted our son to grow up here, in the United States."

"Of course," Chloe acknowledged, hesitating. "But what about Guthrie? Did he know you'd come back?"

He shook his head. "No—we'd changed our names, phony ID. After years of hiding, you pick up some tricks. Even Josh took a pseudonym while he was in Europe so there'd be no connection." He looked at Sara, and his chest moved with a deep breath. "We've been happy here, so happy I guess we got a little careless. Sara even started wearing her hair the way she used to."

"And then I showed up?"

"And then," he said nodding, "you showed up."

Swallowing, Chloe looked at her stepsister. "I didn't know, Sara. I had no idea your father was capable of—"

Sara stopped her with "I know."

"Maybe he's sincere now," Chloe suggested, hope glimmering. "He's been so ill."

"Men like James Guthrie don't change," Rob said bitterly. "He's obsessed with power and control. He can never forget that I took his daughter, and he won't rest until he evens the score. He wants his only grandchild. He wants an heir for the Guthrie dynasty."

Rob's eyes were drawn to the hallway, and Chloe followed them as an adolescent boy appeared, a dark uncertain figure in the pale light. Again, she felt chilled.

"Chloe," Sara said, standing, gesturing for the boy. "This is Evan."

For a moment Chloe could only stare at the dark eyes, young, deep-set, already slightly haunted. "Hello, Evan." She extended her hand. This is *their* son, she told herself. Rob and Sara's.

The strength of his grip surprised her. There was a fierceness, a pride in it. She stepped back, taking in both mother and son, and felt a swell of emotion. The brief look that went between them told her they were united against the world, sharing a bond of love and loyalty beyond anything she'd ever known. The loneliness of her own life struck her, sudden and sharp in contrast. She wanted a beautiful, dark-eyed son like this. She wanted this kind of love.

Evan's tentative voice brought her back. "Sometimes when my mother was homesick she'd tell me about you," he said, sober-eyed, "and about Northpointe." With his mother's shy, serious smile, he added, "She said your hair was fire-red like maple trees in the fall."

Chloe smiled, touched and charmed by his self-consciousness.

As Evan went to stand beside his father, Chloe turned to her sister, her voice softened with emotion. "Sara, I know what you've been through must have been terrible, but it's over now—and you have so much." Tears threatening, she took her sister's hand. "So much to cherish and protect. Please," she whispered, "don't worry. Your father will never find you through me."

Smiling through the tears in her eyes, Sara pressed her cheek to Chloe's and kissed her lightly. "I know, little sister."

The words filled Chloe with gentle waves of pain. The sweet ache of something longed for and finally received ... the sister she'd never had. With a choked sound, Chloe embraced her. "Take care," she whispered. "Take care."

She broke away, managed a trembling smile. "I have to go. There's someone I need to see."

"Is it Nat?" Sara asked. As Chloe nodded, Sara smiled. "Give him our love. And please—tell him we're okay."

Chloe stood at the bow of the ferry, leaning into the railing as though her body weight might propel them forward. "The slow boat to Belmont," she murmured, squinting to see the mainland. "Bet I could swim faster."

Didn't the captain know she had to get back? Didn't he know she needed to be with Nat Cutter again more than she'd ever needed anything in her life? An image took hold in her mind. Looking just the way he always did in her daydreams, she imagined Nat, his hair mussed, eyes shadowed, leaning up against the door frame with that don't-give-a-damn expression on his face.

Just let me at him, she thought, grinning, and I'll make quick work of that cocky look. Riffling through her purse, she found his sunglasses and put them on. A biblical quote came to mind. " 'The truth shall make you free,' " she informed the brisk head wind that was stinging her eyes and blowing her hair.

The truth: Nat Cutter was not the man Sara had run away with. He was free, available, *unencumbered*. The urge to sing out loud came over Chloe—love songs, "The Star Spangled Banner"—but she remembered her fellow passengers and thought better of it. If love was a form of insanity, she was definitely over the edge.

She was in her car and well down the road toward the Sunrise motel before she acknowledged the uneasiness in the pit of her stomach. How would Nat react when she told him she'd found Sara? Musing on the best way to break it to him, she realized that if she hadn't seen her stepsister, she might have called Gordon Browne by now and given away something vital.

The thought sobered her. Sara and her family were the one remaining shadow over Chloe's heart. She hoped Sara's Rob was wrong about James Guthrie. He'd been so sure that Guthrie couldn't be trusted.

In her mind, Chloe reviewed the brief hospital meeting with her stepfather and the conversation with Gordon Browne afterward. The uneasiness built, and her thoughts clicked faster, adding up events: Browne's phone call to her room in Maine, his second call to her office in New York, her own vague suspicions she was being followed.

Chloe hit the brake pedal, wheeled right and pulled the car onto the road's shoulder. *Followed?* If that was true, she'd just led them straight to Sara. She flicked off Nat's glasses, dropped them in her lap.

Rob's words to Sara echoed in her mind. *"It's a trap."*

Was it possible she'd been set up? That it had all been staged—even Guthrie's illness—to flush her out and make her act on whatever information she had about Sara?

No, no, that's crazy, she told herself, remembering the frail, desperately ill man she'd visited in the hospital. A man clinging to life isn't driven by revenge. But she remembered Rob's angry words: *He won't rest until he's evened the score.*

She had to get to a phone, call Sara, warn her.

Accelerating down the last winding, deserted stretch of highway, she imagined the horror of trying to tell Cutter what had happened. "If I've ruined everything he's tried so hard to protect," she whispered, "he'll never forgive me."

She saw his black Corvette parked in the motel lot as she drove in. Her heart thudding, she pulled up next to it. In the rush to open the car door and grab for her purse, she hardly noticed the sunglasses as they slipped off her lap.

The car lurched slightly and rolled backward. Instinctively, she wrenched on the hand brake, recoiling from the sickening pop and crack of glass and metal. "Oh, *no*," she rasped, sliding out of the car.

Staring down in mute horror, she saw the sunglasses caught beneath the tire, their grotesquely twisted frames snapped in two.

Twelve

Nat stared at the empty four-poster and combed a hand through his hair. Where was she? He'd tried to call her several times last night from his hotel room and again from the airport just before his flight back today. Still wearing his raincoat, he looked around the room for a note or some other clue to her whereabouts.

The empty room revealed nothing, no note, no forgotten clothing. He shrugged out of his raincoat, threw it over a chair. She'd shown up night before last with nothing but the clothes she was wearing and her purse. But then, remembering, he turned to the coffee table. *And that book of his poetry.*

The small volume was there, where she'd left it.

He picked it up, leafed through, a hollow sensation in his chest. Something was wrong. He looked around the room again, unable to get the disturbing thought out of his mind. Maybe she'd been called back to New York, he told himself, a business emergency. He picked up the telephone receiver and began to dial. Walt might know.

The desk clerk, with his typical brevity, told Nat he'd seen Chloe pulling out in her rental car the night before. "Ain't seen her since," he added.

Nat's hand tightened on the receiver. "Thanks, Walt." The dial tone buzzed in his head as he stared at the empty bed. She's gone, he thought, finding it hard to breathe. God, *why*? There's so much to tell her.

Muffled sounds caught his attention, the hurried noise of someone approaching. He turned just as the door swung open, and Chloe burst in. His relief at seeing her evaporated as she hesitated on the threshold, her clothes wrinkled and misshapen. A dirt smudge darkened her chin.

"Chloe, what—?"

She moved toward him, her hands cradling something he couldn't see. "Nat," she said, her voice breaking, "I'm sorry."

"What's wrong?" He dropped the phone back into its cradle and went to her. She was holding a pair of shattered glasses that he recognized as his own. Blood oozed from an open cut on her finger. "What happened? An accident? Were you hurt?" Up close, he immediately saw she'd been through some kind of hell. Her eyes were shadowed, her skin waxen.

"No—" she shook her head "—the car—" Swallowing hard, she lost the words, brushed past him to the table and set the glasses down. "I have to call Sara."

He caught her hand as she reached for the phone. "Hold it—what do you mean, call Sara? How do you know about Sara?"

"I found her." She drew herself up as though trying to rein in her emotions. "I found them, Nat—Sara, Rob,

Evan, on the island. They told me everything." She stared up into his eyes. "I know."

He searched her ashen face, disbelief mounting. "You found them? How?"

"Nat," she said warningly, her voice trembling, "let me use the phone."

The conflict in her eyes confused him. There was something she wasn't telling him. "Not until you tell me what's going on. Why do you have to call her?"

Her jaw rigid, she blurted, "I think Guthrie's been having me followed. I think—" she broke off, stiffened "—that he's been using me to find Sara, and I may have played right into his hands." She tried to twist away. "Don't you understand? I left their place nearly two hours ago. It may already be too late!"

She wrenched out of his grip and lunged for the phone, gasping as he blocked her with his arm. "Stop it, Chloe," he warned, catching her wrist as she tried to push him out of the way. In the tangled rush, they jarred up against the table and sent the phone crashing to the floor.

"What's wrong with you?" she snapped, her eyes flashing. "I have to warn her!"

"No." He jerked her away from the table and swung her around to face him. "No, you don't. Listen to me. *James Guthrie is telling the truth.*"

"What?"

"He's an old man who doesn't want to die alone. He's trying to find Sara and make amends."

Her narrowing eyes said she was fast reaching the point of trusting no one, including him. "I don't understand. How do you know that? How can you possibly know Guthrie's motives? No." She shook her head, still trying to twist away. "No, Rob thinks it's a trap.

"Give me a chance, Chloe, please?" He released her wrist and exhaled hard. This was not the way he'd planned to tell her. "I paid James Guthrie a visit this morning—in his hotel suite at the Plaza."

"Met with Guthrie? Why?"

"To check out your story." He saw her flinch. "It wasn't you I didn't trust, it was Guthrie. When you told me he wanted to reconcile with Sara, I figured he was using you as bait."

"And now you're saying he wasn't?"

"That's right, he wasn't. He had Browne keep tabs on you, but only because he suspected you knew something you weren't telling him. But he's not into retribution this time, Chloe. He's sincere about wanting to make up with his daughter." Nat could see she didn't believe it any more than he had at first.

"How can you be sure of that?"

She was holding her wrist where he'd caught her, his finger imprints still visible. He'd hurt her. His jaw tightening, he resisted the impulse to take her hand and caress away the remaining redness. She clearly wasn't ready to let him touch her yet. "I've got it in writing, witnessed by attorneys. Mine and his."

She released a breath, and he began to see the tension ease out of her as he continued. "I didn't believe anything could change James Guthrie, even a brush with death, so I made the preliminary contact with him anonymously, through my attorney in New York. Once my attorney was convinced Guthrie was telling the truth, we set up a meeting."

"That's what you were doing in New York? What about the negotiations, the book contract?"

"That was all true—"

"But you conveniently left out the part about Guthrie. Why didn't you tell me?"

"I couldn't without giving everything away—my own identity, Sara and Rob's cover. Until I knew what Guthrie was up to, I couldn't take that risk."

Hurt flickered. "Why not?" she said indignantly. "What did you think I would do, call *60 Minutes*? I could have helped you."

The smudge on her chin distracted him. She's a mess, he thought, an adorable mess. With that wild red hair she could be one of the orphans in *Annie*. But her round, serious green eyes meant business. They demanded a full accounting.

He shook his head. "The James Guthrie I knew was a ruthless man. He wouldn't have stopped at anything, including having Gordon Browne, or one of his other goons intimidate the truth out of you. I couldn't take that risk until I'd checked him out." He hesitated, stirred by the same protective urge toward her that had once threatened him. "And I couldn't put you in that kind of jeopardy."

She looked thoughtful, and after a moment softened. "What's going to happen now?"

"That's up to Sara and Rob. Guthrie's agreed to let them make the first move. He understands they'll need time."

"Time?" She glanced down at the broken sunglasses. "I'm not sure it's that easy. There might never be enough time for Rob to forgive him."

"Maybe not," he agreed, resignation and sadness in his voice as he acknowledged that possibility. "But at least they have nothing to fear from him now."

They both lapsed into silence as she stared down at the sunglasses. "Looking pretty bad, aren't they?" she said finally, touching the Carreras' cracked lenses. "The work of a world-class klutz. Sorry." Blinking away what might have been tears, she murmured to herself, "Especially since I nearly killed myself getting them off that piling."

"A klutz, maybe," he said laughing, tenderness in his voice. "But a persistent one." He drew her around and looked into eyes that shimmered like emerald chips. "You found your stepsister. Do you realize that you did in one week what Guthrie and his goons couldn't do in fourteen years?"

She began to brighten, a slow-growing inner radiance that took his breath away.

"I had some help," she admitted, catching back a smile. "You. Nobody else saw you but me. They didn't know they should have been looking for two men—or that one of them was named Joshua." Hesitating, lashes lowering briefly, she emitted a breathy sound that confused and excited him. "What do I call you now?" she asked, looking up. "Nat? Josh?"

"Call me Cutter," he said, a slow grin breaking. "Everybody else does."

In the glance that passed between them, he felt something unexpected and wonderful, an uprush of anticipation.

She reached up to touch his face, startling his heart to a rapid beat. "Cutter," she said, rising up on tiptoes to kiss him. As her mouth moved under his, he felt a sliding sensation in his stomach, a weakness that spread to his thighs. Leaning back into the table, he pulled her up against him and shuddered at her warmth and softness. She was a spring flood of sweetness . . . and he was a drowning man.

Their kiss went on, gentle, achingly passionate, until she broke it and pulled back. She didn't say a word, just looked at him as no woman had ever looked at him before.

The desire to take her to bed was like a surge of near pain inside him, but he fought it back, unwilling to break the moment. "I missed you," he said finally, when he could manage the words. His hands on her throat, he caressed her jawline with his thumbs. "Truth is, I was scared out of my mind when I got back here and couldn't find you. For one crazy moment, I thought you'd skipped out on me, gone back to New York."

"Really?" she responded, obviously delighted.

"Really." He brushed at the smudge on her chin with his thumb. "What do I call *you* now? Sherlock?"

She smiled and winked. "Firebreather."

He felt a quick rush of stimulation and urged her closer, sliding his fingers into her hair. "Works for me," he said, grinning.

He'd just begun to kiss her, really kiss her when she murmured, "Wait a minute," pushed out of his arms and looked around the room. "Where's the television?"

"The what?"

"It just occurred to me this very minute. The television you claimed you were listening to at three in the morning when I heard a woman in your room. Where is it?"

He grinned and folded his arms. "On second thought, maybe Sherlock *is* more apt."

"Don't mess with me, Cutter." A fierceness sparked in her eyes.

Damn, she's cute, he thought, and knew if he told her she'd go off like a firecracker. "I had an unexpected visit from Sara that night. She and Rob had been arguing about her father. Sara's wanted to contact him ever since they returned to the States. She thought maybe I could help her convince Rob, but when I took my brother's side, well—" he hesitated, raised a shoulder "—you heard it. She got pretty upset."

Chloe was nodding, pacing, putting things together. "And the man I saw coming out of your room, the one I followed, that was Rob?"

"The FBI could use a good woman like you."

She didn't seem to have heard him. Stopping at the coffee table, she picked up the volume of his poems, hesitated, then turned around to look at him. "'Innocence of Heart'? Did you write it for me?"

She looked so expectant that he sobered. He hadn't, not consciously, but maybe...? "Yeah, it was you."

She nodded, her eyes filling, sparkling. "I knew it." With a long sigh and a heartbreaking smile, she said, "I want to go back there, Cutter. To Northpointe, to the bridge."

The bridge. Joshua Whitney? He'd been afraid of this ever since the night she told him about Sara's disappearance. A flash of pain surrounded his heart. She was clutching the book just as she had that night, like it held some precious, inviolable memory.

I don't remember the old house being this beautiful, Chloe thought, gazing at the red brick of Northpointe through the latticed, sun-drenched bowers of the bridge. She inhaled the nostalgic scent of mossy rocks, gurgling creek water, green trees and sunshine. Her heart full, she could almost believe she'd been happy here.

Turning to see where Nat had gone, she found him standing near the creek bed, staring into the water. A windy gust rustled the tree branches above him and sprinkled him with light and shadows.

Beautiful, she thought, *haunted*. Was she imagining the darkness in him? Watching him turn to stare into the distance, she thought of the myth, and for one enchanted second, she could almost imagine him raising his arms like some marvelous force of nature, splitting the heavens.

She turned away, inexplicably disturbed. Her heart heavy, she realized what must be bothering him. He was trying to find a way to tell her he couldn't continue the relationship. She should have realized that a man like him, a writer, moody and complicated as he was, wouldn't want to be committed. He'd already had one disastrous marriage—

Her thoughts strayed to the day before when she'd asked him to come to Northpointe with her. She thought she'd seen it then, his subtle withdrawal. He'd agreed to go, but said he had to talk with Sara and Rob first. So they'd gone to the island together.

She would never forget the obvious love and surprise in Rob's eyes when he opened the door and embraced his brother. And later, when Nat confirmed what Chloe had already told them about Guthrie, Chloe watched and listened quietly, poignantly aware of the mutual caring and respect the three of them shared.

When Evan entered and went to stand by his uncle, Chloe saw how they were linked, the four of them, by something even more intimate than blood. History, a saga that started at Northpointe. I was there, too, she thought, her heart surging softly. In some way maybe I'm a part of it all.

By the time she and Nat left, Rob had agreed to take Sara and Evan to visit Guthrie. And the healing had begun....

Chloe sighed, a bittersweet sound. A shadow crossed the wooden planks in front of her. She looked up and Nat was there, an arm's length from her. She hadn't imagined the darkness. His features whispered with it.

"Can we talk?" he said.

She leaned into the rail for support. "Yes."

"I think I envy you," he said after a moment. "You've obviously come to terms with your past. You're here, facing it, reexperiencing the good feelings, putting the others to rest."

Awareness came gradually, a heavy thud in her chest. Elena, of course. Was that going to be his reason, that he hadn't resolved the situation with Elena? "And you haven't come to terms with yours?"

"My past?" He hesitated. "No, it's not *my* past that's bothering me, it's yours...or rather, ours."

"I don't understand."

His voice was low and deliberate. "I'm not the man you're remembering, Chloe. The one who carried you to this bridge."

"Joshua? You're not him? Then who—?"

"No—" He raised a hand, his eyes asking her to understand. "I mean I lost Joshua Whitney a long time ago. Too much has happened, too many shattered illusions. Men like him, full of dreams, they don't survive in this world."

He broke off and exhaled. "I know you loved him, but if you came back here hoping you'd rediscover him, that I'd suddenly be him again..."

Whatever it was he said next got lost in the whirling sensation in her brain. "Do you mean that's it?" she whispered through a dizzy, giddy little tornado of insight. "That's what's been bothering you? You thought I was trying to recapture that past, the love I might have felt for Joshua?"

He considered her, puzzled. "Yeah...you weren't?"

"Oh, Cutter," she breathed, sagging against the railing. "I thought you were going to tell me you didn't want a relationship, that the artist in you couldn't be confined—" She broke off, looked up at him. "You weren't coming to that next, were you?"

The glint in his eyes unnerved her. Wicked, she thought, easily the closest approximation of sheer wickedness she'd ever seen in her life. She felt a pulse quicken in her throat. "Don't mess with me, Cutter."

He caught the collar of her blouse, dragged her closer. "No, I wasn't coming to that next. I was just wondering if you've considered what you'd be getting into. You and me,

I mean. I'm hell to live with—cynical, stubborn, given to moods—"

"True," she breathed, dizzy from the nearness of him. "But you're also gentle and funny—" she felt her face flushing "—and you make love like a god."

With a husky sound, he pulled her to him. "I leave my clothes lying around," he confessed, breathtakingly near her lips. "I stay up all night writing."

"All true," she agreed again, tidying the hair that curled onto his temples, the thrill of touching him tingling down her arm, "but I think I can train you."

His soft growl of laughter kindled a fire inside her. She pressed her fingers to his mouth, anticipating his protest. "No more excuses. I want you, Nathanial Cutter, I want your dark-eyed babies."

He sobered instantly, a shudder passing through him. Holding her face, he kissed her with such unbridled passion that she saw starbursts in her head. His hunger aroused her; the connection their bodies made thrilled her to her soul.

The kiss deepened, echoing through them, gentling to breathy, nerve-spun tremors. Trembling in its wake they held each other, silenced by emotion. Sunlight poured over them, soft and golden, and Chloe knew in her heart that she'd finally come home.

Through the mist in her eyes, she looked up at him, and tried to smile. "I adore you, Cutter, I always have."

She saw the miracle happening inside him, felt its power. He caressed her face, obviously shaken. "I wish I could tell you what I'm feeling—" his voice caught "—but there aren't words."

"I know," she said. "I know."

And then, suddenly, as though something had broken free inside him, he whispered, "I love you."

He said it again, touched her face, and Chloe felt a moment of inexpressible rapture, like the crescendo of a symphonic chord inside her. Her heart was beating everywhere, in her own hand as she pressed it over his, in the air around them, in the covering bowers of the bridge.

Her world hesitated in its orbit, waiting, shimmering, caught like the hand of a clock between seconds. "I love you," she whispered, hearing the peal of soft chimes. Time had begun again. The world was new.

Afterword

On the last morning in June, an unsurpassingly beautiful summer day, Chloe Katherine Kates married Joshua Whitney beneath the sun-drenched bowers of the old bridge at Northpointe. Rob and Sara Whitney were in attendance with their son, Evan.

One year later, Chloe and Joshua had their first child, a boy.

ATTRACTIVE, SPACE SAVING BOOK RACK

Display your most prized novels on this handsome and sturdy book rack. The hand-rubbed walnut finish will blend into your library decor with quiet elegance, providing a practical organizer for your favorite hard-or soft-covered books.

Only $9.95

Approximately 16" x 8" when assembled

Assembles in seconds!

To order, rush your name, address and zip code, along with a check or money order for $10.70* ($9.95 plus 75¢ postage and handling) payable to *Silhouette Books*.

Silhouette Books
Book Rack Offer
901 Fuhrmann Blvd.
P.O. Box 1325
Buffalo, NY 14269-1325

Offer not available in Canada.

*New York residents add appropriate sales tax.

BKR-2R

Silhouette Desire

**Available
January 1987**

NEVADA
SILVER

The third book in the exciting
Desire Trilogy by Joan Hohl.

The Sharp brothers are back, along with
sister Kit... and Logan McKittrick.

Kit's loved Logan all her life and, with a little
help from the silver glow of a Nevada night,
she must convince the stubborn rancher that
she's a woman who needs a man's love—not
the protection of another brother.

Don't miss *Nevada Silver*—Kit and
Logan's story and the conclusion
of Joan Hohl's acclaimed
Desire Trilogy.

FOUR UNIQUE SERIES
FOR EVERY WOMAN YOU ARE...

Silhouette Romance

Heartwarming romances that will make you laugh and cry as they bring you all the wonder and magic of falling in love.

6 titles per month

Silhouette Special Edition

Expanded romances written with emotion and heightened romantic tension to ensure powerful stories. A rare blend of passion and dramatic realism.

6 titles per month

Silhouette Desire

Believable, sensuous, compelling—and above all, romantic—these stories deliver the promise of love, the guarantee of satisfaction.

6 titles per month

Silhouette Intimate Moments

Love stories that entice; longer, more sensuous romances filled with adventure, suspense, glamour and melodrama.

4 titles per month

Silhouette Romances
not available in retail outlets in Canada

SIL-GEN-1A

Take 4 Silhouette
Intimate Moments novels
FREE

Then preview 4 brand new Silhouette Intimate Moments® novels
—delivered to your door every month—for 15 days as soon as
they are published. When you decide to keep them, you pay just
$2.25 each ($2.50 each, in Canada), *with no shipping, handling, or other charges of any kind!*

Silhouette Intimate Moments novels are not for everyone.
They were created to give you a more detailed, more exciting
reading experience, filled with romantic fantasy, intense sensuality, and stirring passion.

The first 4 Silhouette Intimate Moments novels are absolutely
FREE and without obligation, yours to keep. You can cancel at
any time.

You'll also receive a FREE subscription to the Silhouette Books
Newsletter as long as you remain a member. Each issue is filled
with news on upcoming titles, interviews with your favorite
authors, even their favorite recipes.

To get your 4 FREE books, fill out and mail the coupon today!

Silhouette Intimate Moments®

Silhouette Books, 120 Brighton Rd., P.O. Box 5084, Clifton, NJ 07015-5084